His eyes glinted with amusement.

"Miss Lucinda Bliss," he said solemnly, "will you do me the very great honor of bestowing on me your hand in marriage?"

"Yes," Lucy said coldly.

He rose to his feet and drew her into his arms and bent his mouth to kiss her, but she jerked away and the kiss landed somewhere near her ear. He laughed and took her chin in his hand and held her firm. Then he kissed her mouth, warmly and sweetly, finally drawing back to leave her breathless and trembling.

"I see I do not leave your senses unaffected," he said. Lucy wiped her mouth with the back of her hand and glared at him. Her knees were shaking. How on earth was she going to win the battle if he was going to kiss her like that . . . ?

Also by Marion Chesney
Published by Fawcett Books:

REGENCY GOLD
THE CONSTANT COMPANION
LADY MARGEY'S INTRIGUE
MY LORDS, LADIES AND MARJORIE
QUADRILLE
LOVE AND LADY LOVELACE
THE GHOST AND LADY ALICE
THE DUKE'S DIAMONDS
LADY LUCY'S LOVER
THE FRENCH AFFAIR
MINERVA
SWEET MASQUERADE
THE TAMING OF ANNABELLE
DEIRDRE AND DESIRE
THE FLIRT
DAPHNE
THOSE ENDEARING YOUNG CHARMS
TO DREAM OF LOVE
DIANA THE HUNTRESS
AT THE SIGN OF THE GOLDEN PINEAPPLE
FREDRICA IN FASHION
MILADY IN LOVE
LESSONS IN LOVE
THE PAPER PRINCESS
THE PERFECT GENTLEMAN
PRETTY POLLY
THE FIRST REBELLION
SILKEN BONDS
THE LOVE MATCH
THE SCANDALOUS LADY WRIGHT
HIS LORDSHIP'S PLEASURE
HER GRACE'S PASSION

THE SCANDALOUS MARRIAGE

Marion Chesney

FAWCETT CREST • NEW YORK

A Fawcett Crest Book
Published by Ballantine Books
 Published in the United States by Ballantine Books, a division of Random House, Inc., New York, and simultaneously in Canada by Random House of Canada Limited, Toronto.

Library of Congress Catalog Card Number: 91-75835

ISBN 0-449-21992-5

Manufactured in the United States of America

First Edition: February 1992

Chapter One

LUCY BLISS SLIPPED quietly out of her home to walk in the grounds and get away from the sound of her mother's voice. Mrs. Bliss had gone into her husband's study, and steady nagging recriminations sounded through the house.

It was a February day, fresh and chilly, with a light breeze rustling through the leaves of the evergreens bordering the drive.

If I ever get a home of my own, thought Lucy, I shall have a garden full of flowers and deciduous trees. No evergreens.

Mrs. Bliss liked evergreens. They were so neat and tidy and did not shed their leaves in autumn in a messy way. Only one part of the extensive gardens of Dove House, the Bliss family home, had been left in a wild state, and it was there Lucy always went when she was troubled.

Her mother usually nagged on and on when she wanted something; there was nothing unusual about that. But Lucy could not help feeling a sense of dread, a sense that her life was about to change for the worse and that her mother's nagging had something to do with it.

She was nineteen years old and had not made her come-out. Nor had any debut been suggested. Lucy knew her mother was sadly disappointed in her elder daughter's looks and considered a Season a waste of time and money. But Belinda, Lucy's younger sister, was another matter. She had just turned seventeen and had put her hair up for the first time. The Bliss sisters had attended a local assembly two nights ago, and Belinda had been mobbed by gentlemen, Belinda with her curly brown-gold hair and huge blue eyes and plump little figure. Lucy, as usual, had sat on a chair against the wall, ignored. She knew her looks were unfortunate. Her hair was silvery-fair, fine and wispy, and her eyes of clear gray too large for her thin face. She was slim and small-breasted, both sad defects in an age when plumpness in a female was admired.

Not that Lucy was jealous of her pretty sister. Rather, she was protective of her. Lucy had not liked the way Mrs. Bliss had preened herself as she had watched Belinda's success at the assembly, nor the way she had whispered loudly to a friend, "She is wasted on such country bumpkins. Why, she could marry a duke." The friend had leaned towards Mrs. Bliss and had begun to mutter urgently, and Mrs. Bliss's eyes had begun to glow. Since then, it became obvious to Lucy that Mrs. Bliss wanted something that her normally shy and retiring husband was not prepared to give her. Hence the constant nagging.

In the wild part of the garden little clumps of snowdrops were poking up through the shaggy grass under the trees, "real trees" here, as Lucy thought, birch and alder which would soon bear the tender green leaves of spring. The wind gently rocked the branches, and on the ground, little white heads of the snowdrops bobbed and nodded.

Lucy wondered what it would be like to be married. She would have a home of her own, and children, and she could ask Belinda to live with her, away from Mrs. Bliss's ambitions. That was it, thought Lucy, what she had really known since the assembly. Mrs. Bliss's ambitions for Belinda had been fired, and whatever they were, gentle Belinda would not have strength to stand up to her mother.

The day was cold, and Lucy shivered and drew her cloak more tightly about her shoulders. She would have liked to be able to return to the house with the prospect of sitting peacefully in front of a blazing fire. But there was never anywhere she could go where her mother would not find her. Other young misses of Lucy's rank barely saw either of their parents, being closer to their nurserymaids and their governesses. But for as long as Lucy could remember, her mother supervised every inch of her life and her sister's. There had been a governess, a gentle creature, who had recently been dismissed "because the girls know enough." But while she had been teaching the girls, Mrs. Bliss had been present at the lessons. Lucy's mother appeared to have boundless energy.

The cold of the day eventually forced her to turn her reluctant footsteps toward the house. It was a large, square, brick building, built in the time of Queen Anne. No vulgar ivy had been allowed to soften its uncompromising lines.

Mr. Bliss hailed from the untitled aristocracy. His wife came from one rung down on the social ladder, the gentry. He was a quiet, scholarly man who sometimes regretted the day he had married his wife. But she had been so pretty, so complacent, so gentle, just like her daughter Belinda appeared at present. How was he to know that she would develop into one of society's most vulgar and formidable matrons?

And there, as Lucy entered the highly polished hall, was that matron.

Mrs. Bliss was enveloped in a purple silk gown. It was strained over her ample bosom and hips. Her round cheeks were highly rouged, and her once beautiful eyes had become small and beady. "There you are, Lucy," she declared, "and out walking in this inclement weather again. You will ruin your complexion. Not that I have high hopes for you, but you will make an excellent clergyman's wife if you play your cards right. Well, it is all settled; although Mr. Bliss proved amazingly stubborn, I quite overcame him with good sense. The minute Mrs. Cartwright said that Wardshire was to go to the Season, I knew plain where my duty lay. You are looking uncommonly stupid, Lucy. I mean the Duke of Wardshire."

"I know who you mean, Mama," said Lucy faintly. "Lucifer Wardshire."

"Servants' tittle-tattle. He is one of the richest men in the kingdom, and he can only be going to the Season for one reason—to find a bride. He must meet Belinda. We must be in London very soon, for I must arrange all the necessary connections to launch Belinda. Her clothes must be of the first stare."

"Mama," protested Lucy, "Wardshire is an *old man*. He is all of thirty-four. Belinda is *seventeen*. He also has a foul reputation. 'Tis said he has *or-*

gies at his home. 'Tis said he has sold his soul to the devil. 'Tis—"

"Pooh! It is a good thing my ambitions do not rest on *you*, Lucy. We are to leave for London at the end of the week."

Lucy looked bewildered. "But the packing, the arranging . . ."

"Nothing to it. I had this in mind for some time, and to that end visited your Uncle George. He never uses his town house, and it is a most genteel address. The last time I visited him, I persuaded him to give me the keys. The servants will go ahead and put all in order. Your dresses will be made in London, for I will not have anyone saying my daughters look provincial."

Lucy started to mount the stairs, hoping to get to the sanctuary of her room, to think things out, but as usual, her mother followed her. Mrs. Bliss wore a very powerful perfume. It seemed to envelop Lucy in a great yellow cloud.

A footman stood aside to let them pass. "James," said Mrs. Bliss, "fetch Miss Belinda and bring her to Miss Lucy's bedchamber."

Lucy groaned inwardly. No time to rest and think.

As she took off her hat and Mrs. Bliss plumped herself down in an armchair by the fire, Belinda came into the room.

"My pet! My precious!" exclaimed Mrs. Bliss. "Such a future your mama has planned for you! You are to wed the Duke of Wardshire."

Belinda flushed in surprise and amazement. "When did he propose?"

"Silly puss. He has not proposed *yet*, but he will. We are to go to London, and there you will meet him. Your gowns must be by, let me think, Farré, and . . ."

Her voice rose and fell remorselessly. When the dressing bell rang, she continued to talk on and so the sisters ended up changing their gowns in a scramble in order to get to the dinner table on time.

Mrs. Bliss talked on through dinner while her husband sat, gray and silent. Then to the drawing room. Lucy was commanded to entertain them on the pianoforte, and behind her, as she played, her mother's voice rose and fell in a sort of counterpoint.

The supper tray was brought in. Mrs. Bliss had the rare ability of managing to enunciate every word with her mouth full. Lucy unscrewed one pearl earring from her left ear and then screwed it back in again. Pierced ears were for savages, so her earrings were fastened with little screws which pressed into the lobe. Belinda saw the action and gave a slight nod. The sisters had developed a series of movements that could be translated into various messages. The unscrewing of the left earring was Lucy's signal to her sister to come to her bedchamber when their parents were asleep.

At last Lucy was able to escape. Her maid undressed her and then Lucy climbed into bed, hoping Belinda would not fall asleep before Mrs. Bliss did. Lucy also hoped the excited Mrs. Bliss would not come in as she often did and sit chattering on the end of the bed until all hours. Lucy often fantasized about gagging her mother for one whole day, just to hear the silence.

She lay awake for a long time until she heard her parents mounting the stairs, her mother talking on and on and her father answering in mumbles. Poor Papa, thought Lucy, not for the first time. What kind of man was he under the gray exterior? Did he, too, often dream of freedom? Or had he become too crushed by his wife's domineering personality to have any independent thought at all?

Silence fell on the house, blessed deep silence. Then, to Lucy's relief, the door opened gently and Belinda slipped quietly in.

"What are we going to do?" asked Lucy.

"Do?" echoed Belinda.

"I mean, about your marrying the duke."

Belinda wrinkled her brow. "Well, you know, sis, it would be no very bad thing to be a duchess. And you could come and live with me. I've got to marry someone. Can you imagine being left an old maid?"

"Easily," said Lucy dryly. "With a less noisy parent, I could look forward to that future with great equanimity. But, Belinda, this duke is old and a monster. He has orgies."

Belinda looked at her doubtfully. "But is that not the way of men, Lucy? They are such very coarse, violent creatures, you know, and we have to accept that. Besides," she went on, "all I have to do is produce an heir and then this duke will leave me alone and go back to his orgies and mistresses."

"Belinda, by the time such a man is finished with you, you would be broken in spirit."

"Do you think so?" Belinda looked at her sister placidly. "You know, Lucy, neither you or Mama appear to have stopped to think that this duke may not want me." She giggled. "I overheard Mrs. Belize saying at the assembly that Mama was the most pushing and vulgar woman she had ever met. Just think, Lucy! Mrs. Belize said that, and she is only a lawyer's wife. So what will a grand and noble duke make of Mama?"

Lucy fell back against the pillows and laughed and laughed. Then she wiped her streaming eyes. "What a sensible girl you are, Belinda, and I have been worrying myself to flinders. You have the right of it. Meanwhile, surely in London Mama will be busy making calls and things and have less time to *talk* to us. Perhaps we might be able to see some of the unfashionable sights. Feathers"—Feathers was their lady's maid—"was saying this night that she planned to see the wild beasts at the Tower of London. And we shall meet other young people, and young men, too. Not some superannuated horror of a duke."

The Duke of Wardshire was at that moment sitting by a large fire in his library drinking brandy with his friend, the Honorable Rufus Graham. Mr. Graham was a Scotchman, indolent and easygoing. He dressed in what he prided himself was the latest fashion, which meant everything about his slim figure was too padded and too tight, and his pantaloons were molded to his long, slim legs like those of a ballet dancer. His amiable, sheeplike face surveyed the duke over a starched cravat of stunning intricacy and hellish discomfort. The duke was in his undress: a banyan worn over shirt and breeches and slippers. Mr. Graham, on the other hand, felt that a gentleman should never be seen minus starch, corsets, padding, and coat except by his valet, a few minutes before going to bed.

"So you are thinking of getting married?" asked Mr. Graham.

"Perhaps," said the duke laconically. He was a

tall man with jet black hair, a hawklike face, and pale silvery eyes, and looked like the Lucifer he was reputed to be.

Mr. Graham looked amused. "And what, then, of this reputation you have so carefully built up? Faith! Do you remember when Lady Jasper came to call with a carriageful of daughters and you got me dressed up in red wig and gown to receive them and pretend I was your mistress? Ah, but we were young then."

"We are hardly in our dotage now," pointed out the duke. "From time to time my servants spread gossip that I have a house full of doxies, and that seems enough to keep ambitious mamas at bay."

"But how will you now *unmake* your reputation?" asked his friend curiously. "What if you fall in love with some pretty innocent at the Season?"

"Love? I? My friend, you grow mawkish. I do not need to worry about my reputation. I am rich and titled and will find it easy to pick out a wife. I have a mind to have children."

"Don't the females have a say in that?"

"You are become squeamish. I know what it is. Spring is nearly upon us and you grow sentimental and think of romance for yourself. We shall enjoy ourselves in London. I have been in the country too long and am become the veriest rustic."

"Have you considered," said Mr. Graham, "that you might become enamored of a female who don't want you? After all, what about Lady Fortescue . . . ?"

The duke's eyes flashed with temper. "Clarinda Bellington, now Lady Fortescue, turned me down when I was a green army captain. How was that ladybird to know I would inherit a dukedom? No, the ladies fall in love with rank and fortune, just the way their mothers have schooled them to."

"Well, it's a hard world for the ladies," pointed out the softhearted Mr. Graham. "Marriage is a career. Love don't enter into it. We can join the military or the church, but what can they do else?"

"They could in many cases settle for love and less, but that has not been my experience."

"Lady Fortescue embittered you, and that's a fact," said Mr. Graham. "When I heard two years ago she was a widow, I thought you might try your luck again."

"Hardly, my friend. I do have my pride. How does she look?"

"Very beautiful. She does not seem to have aged."

The duke fell silent. He remembered Clarinda vividly. He remembered the sweet spring evening in the garden of her parents' home when she had let him steal a kiss. How elated he had been as he had walked away, promising to see her on his next leave. How many dreams he had dreamed of her as he had fought on the high sierras of Spain. But in his absence, she had made her come-out in London and had taken the town by storm. By the time he had returned, she had married the rich and elderly Lord Fortescue, and he had found himself Duke of Wardshire due to the death of the late duke's nearer relatives in a smallpox epidemic. He had also found himself much sought after. He was rated the highest prize on the marriage market. Sickened, he had retreated to the country only to find out that determined mothers and fathers followed him there, and so he had begun to build up a horrible reputation for himself so as to live in peace. He had occasionally traveled to Italy and had enjoyed the society of

Rome and Venice, but he had never returned to London.

It had only been recently that he had begun to yearn, not for love, but for a son. To that end he had ordered the town house to be opened up and aired and dusted. Mr. Graham watched the duke's face and suddenly wished that somewhere in London the duke would come across just one female who would not be impressed by his title. But he doubted it. He had just traveled down from London himself, and society was already humming with the news that the duke's town house was being prepared for his forthcoming visit. All the duke's wicked reputation was being put down by the hopeful as nothing more than malicious gossip. But he did not tell the duke that, because he wanted to enjoy a leisurely visit and did not want to rouse the duke into planning anything to reinforce his bad reputation.

"Even if you don't find a bride," said Mr. Graham, "it will do you good to get about a bit and enjoy some plays and operas and meet some decent English people. Italian society is not the same."

"No," agreed the duke. "It was much more enjoyable."

"I suppose," went on Mr. Graham, "you will be having some callers soon."

"Why?"

"Well, the local county will now know the news, and some of the mamas will want to be ahead of the game."

"Let them try," said the duke, looking amused. "I have no mind to socialize until I get to town."

Mrs. Bliss bustled into Lucy's bedroom the following morning and awoke her sleeping daughter by jerking back the curtains and flooding the bedchamber with chilly gray light. "You must rouse yourself, my pet," ordered Mrs. Bliss. "Two in the afternoon will be a good time to call, I think, and it will take all that time to get you ready. You girls must wear those sweet muslins. A trifle provincial, I fear, but let's hope he does not notice. Mr. Bliss is being most stubborn and refuses to accompany us. What ails the man? Does he not want to see his daughters wed?"

Lucy struggled up. "Where are we going?"

"Why, to call on Wardshire, of course."

"But I thought we were going to London with that in mind. Everyone in the county knows he doesn't receive callers, not even the Lord Lieutenant, not even the bishop. We shall be most dreadfully snubbed."

"Fiddle! Faint heart never won fair gentleman. Bustle about. Feathers! The pink sprig for Miss Lucy and the rose sprig for Miss Belinda, and those new bonnets with the flowers."

Lucy shivered as she climbed down from the high bed and went to the window and looked out. Gray, ragged clouds were hurtling across the sky, and rods of sleet were stabbing into the lawn below. "Muslin, Mama, in such weather. We shall die of the ague."

"You must suffer to be beautiful, or rather Belinda must. My hopes are pinned on Belinda, but there is no need for *you* to look like a guy. Heat the curling tongs, Feathers, and see what you can do with Miss Lucy's hair."

Lucy knew from experience that it was useless to argue with her mother. She would just need to shiver in muslin on the drive to the duke's home, Sarsey, wait to be rebuffed, and shiver on the road back.

How ridiculous they looked, thought Lucy as they set out that afternoon. Mrs. Bliss was attired in a gold silk gown and silk pelisse trimmed with fur. On her head was a tall-crowned felt hat embellished with pheasants' feathers. Lucy and Belinda were wearing their thin muslins, each barely protected from the cold with a cashmere shawl. On their heads were straw bonnets bedecked with flowers, and their feet were encased in the thinnest of kid slippers.

Lucy found her heart was beginning to beat a little faster as their carriage turned in at the lodge gates of Sarsey. The sleet was changing to snow. The day was dark and sinister. Above their heads the trees lining the long drive bowed and bent down over them, the bare branches stretched out toward the carriage like skeletal fingers. Belinda shivered and pressed close to Lucy, and Lucy squeezed her hand and gave her a reassuring smile. Soon it would be over, thought Lucy. Their footman would knock at the door and present Mrs. Bliss's card. He would return to say that the duke was "not at home," a polite fiction meaning the duke did not want to see them, and then they could go back. She realized with surprise that her mother was still talking, had not stopped talking since they left home. Mrs. Bliss was speculating how the duke would look when he saw Belinda, and from there she went on easily to plans for a big society wedding and how many noses she would put out of joint with her success.

A large house loomed up, a palace, dark and forbidding and immensely grand. Mrs. Bliss suddenly fell silent, and Lucy wondered whether her mother had at last realized the enormity of what she was doing. But it had suddenly occurred to Mrs. Bliss how easy it would be for the duke not to see them, not even to be aware of their call. He had no doubt told his servants to refuse all callers.

So when the footman let down the carriage steps and then turned to approach the great door to present her card, Mrs. Bliss called him back. "We will go ourselves, John," she said. "I am sure His Grace is expecting us." And ignoring Lucy's startled exclamation of protest, she shooed them from the carriage and herded them before her to the door.

Mrs. Bliss seized the knocker, which was in the shape of a grinning devil's head, and rapped smartly. The door was opened by a reassuringly ordinary butler. He was just inclining his head to murmur politely that the duke was not at home when the duke himself crossed the hall. Mrs. Bliss simply elbowed the butler aside. "Your Grace," she cooed, tripping up to him, silk-covered bosoms bobbing under her open pelisse, "are we not fortunate to find you at home. Come, girls."

The butler looked desperately to his master for help. "I was about to say you were not at home, Your Grace."

"And to all intents and purposes, I am not," said the duke icily. He wrapped his banyan of gold cloth more tightly about his tall figure and stared down from his great height at Mrs. Bliss.

"But you are," exclaimed Mrs. Bliss. "And here we are, being very neighborly. I said to my Belinda, His Grace will be delighted with a little female company." She half turned and grabbed Belinda's arm and dragged her forward. The duke raised his quizzing glass and looked down, not at Belinda, but at Mrs. Bliss. "I do not want a little female company, nor indeed any . . . er . . . *large* female company. Now, if you would be so good—"

He was interrupted by Lucy, who had marched forward and now stood glaring up at him, her fists clenched. Lucy despised her mother but could not bear to see her humiliated by anyone. "Come, Mama," she said, "this whole idea of yours, although well intentioned, was a great mistake. I am cold and miserable and so is Belinda, and you will come home with us before you are more badly snubbed than you already have been."

The duke looked at her in surprise. Her little nose was red with cold, and under her unseasonal straw bonnet, her hair had begun to come out of curl and was lying in wispy tendrils on her cold cheeks. Her large eyes shone with anger.

A sudden spark of amusement lit up his own eyes. "But you did not let me finish. I was about to say, if you will be so good as to step into the library and warm yourselves by the fire, I shall order some refreshment to be sent to you."

"You did not think any such thing," raged Lucy. "You just said that to make me look foolish."

"Thankee," said Mrs. Bliss, ignoring Lucy and urging Belinda toward where a footman was holding open the library door. "So very kind, I'm sure. The weather is so inclement."

The duke stood aside and smiled down at Lucy. "You look very cold," he said in a mocking voice.

In exasperation, Lucy spoke her thoughts aloud. "I don't know which one of you is the worst, Mama with her vulgar pushiness or you with your mockery." Then she blushed to the roots of her hair in mortification as she immediately realized she had spoken her thoughts aloud. "I b-beg your pardon," she said miserably, but he had already turned away and was saying to his hovering butler, "Fetch Mr. Graham. Tell him I have company. And bring negus and cakes to the library."

Lucy walked quickly into the library and sat down by Belinda. "No, not there!" hissed her mother. "He must see Belinda on her own." Lucy was miserably aware that the duke had entered the room just in time to hear this remark.

What a terrifying man he seemed, and how scared poor Belinda looked. Lucy had been inclined to think that a great deal of nonsense had been talked about the wicked duke, but one look at that satanically handsome face was enough to make anyone shiver. Mrs. Bliss launched into speech. "What a fine palace you do have, Duke, but if you don't mind my saying so, it could do with a leetle of the feminine touch."

"I have a housekeeper," remarked the duke.

Mrs. Bliss wagged an arch finger at him. "Naughty! I am persuaded you know just what I mean. We are in such a flurry because Belinda here is to make her come-out and we are going to London. I believe you plan to go yourself. Of course, I doubt if you will even see my Belinda, for at her first ball she will be surrounded by so many courtiers. Oh, I declare. I am that overcome I have not made the introductions. I am Mrs. Bliss of Dove House, and this is my Belinda. Make your curtsy, Belinda. There. Don't she curtsy a treat."

The duke's eyes slid to Lucy. "And is this your daughter's companion?"

"No, no, this is my elder daughter, Lucy . . . Lucinda."

"Ah, therefore Miss Lucy has already made her come-out."

"No, for there was not any reason. But with such beauty as Belinda's, it would be a shame to let her pine unseen in the country."

"Indeed it would," said the duke, his eyes ranging insolently over Belinda's plump and demure figure. He turned as Mr. Graham entered the room and introduced him. The butler and two footmen followed bearing trays carrying a bowl of negus, glasses, and an array of cakes and biscuits.

Mrs. Bliss curtsied low before Mr. Graham, determined to flatter this friend of the duke. As she rose, her eyes slid from Mr. Graham to Lucy, and then one could almost see her thinking that Lucy did not present any hope whatsoever.

"Do you attend many balls and parties in the country?" the duke asked Belinda.

Before Belinda could reply, Mrs. Bliss weighed in. "Wasn't we at the assembly t'other night and wasn't pet here mobbed, but simply mobbed, by the gentlemen? Why, says I, you could marry a duke!" She gave a genteel simper. "What am I saying? My tongue does run on with me."

The duke watched fascinated as negus and cakes were served all round. Mrs. Bliss, he noticed, had mastered the art of eating cream cakes while still talking. "So," went on Mrs. Bliss archly, "I am sure you will be desirous to call on us in London, Your Grace, to get ahead of the game, as it were, if you take my meaning."

"I am afraid I do not understand you," said the duke.

"Mama!" breathed Lucy in an anguished undertone.

"*You* know," said Mrs. Bliss.

"I do not, madam."

"Well, you've seen our Belinda first. So many men will be wanting her hand in marriage."

The duke surveyed Mrs. Bliss in admiration. He had met some pushy parents in his time, but Mrs. Bliss beat them all to flinders.

"I am sorry to disappoint you," he said, "but I will be much engaged in matters of business. But, as you rightly say, your pretty daughters will have no difficulty in finding husbands."

Mrs. Bliss looked disappointed at this momentary setback but then plunged deeper into the mire of social gaffes. "Oh, I am not one of your vulgar ambitious women, Your Grace. Have I hopes for Lucy? No, I have not."

"I cannot understand why," remarked the duke insolently. He put up his glass and studied Lucy.

"She's a sweet girl, but she ain't got what it takes, and that's a fact. But my Belinda—"

The duke wearied of the game. He looked out the window. "I am loath to cut short your visit, madam, but the snow is beginning to lie . . ."

"Think nothing of it," said Mrs. Bliss, settling back in her chair. "We are intrepid travelers."

"I insist," said the duke. He rang the bell, and when a footman answered it, he asked for Mrs. Bliss's carriage to be brought round immediately.

Mrs. Bliss rose, slightly huffed. "My Belinda is a strong girl for all her looks," she remarked. "Good stock."

"But as I pointed out, the snow is still falling," said the duke, "and I do not have time to examine her teeth."

Mr. Graham let out an unmanly snigger, and Lucy glared.

Mrs. Bliss chattered her way into the hall, her

voice beating remorselessly on the air while Lucy felt ready to sink with shame.

Lucy and Belinda sat huddled in the carriage on the road home as their mother crowed over the "success" of the visit. But at last Lucy was able to shut off her mother's voice and reflect that Belinda was well and truly safe now from the sinister Duke of Wardshire. She remembered the look on his face as they had left. Her mother and Belinda were already in the carriage, but Lucy, one foot on the carriage steps, had turned and looked back. The duke's face had been the very picture of mockery mixed with disgust.

"What on earth were you about," Mr. Graham was demanding, "to let such a creature in your home after years of keeping even the nicest at bay? Faugh! She smelled of the shop."

"As far as I know, she comes from an impeccable background," said the duke. "You must have noticed before that the much-maligned shopkeeper often has excellent manners compared to certain ladies of the ton."

"I was sorry for the daughters," commented Mr. Graham. "That Belinda is vastly pretty, but how will she take at the Season with a mother like that?"

"Yes," said the duke thoughtfully. "But I was particularly sorry for the elder girl."

Mr. Graham shrugged. "Waiflike creature, but of no particular style or looks. Let us talk about something else. We are not likely to meet the Bliss family again."

Chapter Two

FOR THE FIRST TIME she could remember, Lucy found peace, and it was amongst the rattle and noise of London. Mrs. Bliss was too occupied with "nursing the ground," which meant she sought invitations to the best houses for her daughters. Some who would have liked to snub her did not, because she seemed to have a hide impenetrable to insult, and so it was easier to give in to her; others, because this vulgar Mrs. Bliss was a friend of the Duke of Wardshire, and all wanted an introduction to him.

Lucy's wardrobe was quickly finished. It had been explained that she could not expect to have as many dresses as her pretty sister. So one bright spring day when Mrs. Bliss was occupied with the dressmaker, busy choosing designs for more gowns for Belinda, and Belinda was kept close to "give her opinion," which meant agreeing to everything her mother said, Lucy asked if she might go out for a drive with Feathers. Absentmindedly Mrs. Bliss murmured "Mmm," which Lucy cheerfully interpreted to mean permission.

Feathers was a tall, angular woman whose austere appearance hid a girlish desire to "visit the lions," current cant for seeing the sights, and so she clapped her hands when Lucy said they should go to the Tower of London to look at the wild beasts.

Almost dizzy with elation at this rare day of freedom, Lucy ordered the open carriage to take them, for the weather was warm and fine. It was hard to remember on such a glorious day that the fickle English spring could change back into winter at any moment. The footman on the backstrap, a tall, gangling country youth called John, had never before seen the sights of London either, and added to the air of excitement as he looked around him, exclaiming at the fine shops and buildings.

The Tower, that great medieval fortress on the banks of the Thames, sobered them. "What a grim place," said Lucy in awe. "A fit setting for the Duke of Wardshire. You should have seen him, Feathers, looking like the devil himself. I can only be happy that Mama gave him such a disgust of us that he would never in a hundred years think of proposing to Belinda."

"I have heard of the duke," said Feathers with a shiver. " 'Tis said he holds the black mass in the family chapel."

Lucy looked at the maid doubtfully. "Although he struck me as a bad man, he did not strike me as being *silly*. And surely only very silly people get up to such theatricals."

"There is no imagining the dreadful things that evil people will get up to," said Feathers grimly. "Oh, here are the beasts."

The stopped and stared into a cage where a mangy lion paced up and down. "I really do not think I am enjoying this," said Lucy as they began to move along the cages. "Such a fine day, and to see these poor creatures in captivity. I declare it is quite depressing. We should have gone to the waxworks instead."

A brightly colored ball rolled along in front of the cages and came to a stop at Lucy's feet. She picked it up and looked around. A small, sturdy boy came running up. Lucy judged him to be about six years old. He was wearing a gown and petticoats and a straw top hat, the usual dress for small boys, who were attired as girls until they reached the age of eight. He had rosy cheeks and periwinkle blue eyes.

"May I have my ball?" he asked. Lucy held it out to him. "Where is your mama?" she asked.

"At home," he replied moodily, starting to bounce the ball up and down.

"Then who is here with you?"

"Old Grizzly Face," he replied. He bounced the ball against a tiger's cage, and the animal inside snarled a moody warning.

"Oh, do be careful," pleaded Lucy. "Let us go and find . . . er . . . Old Grizzly Face. Did you run away from him?"

"Yes, he was giving me a jaw-me-dead about the beasts, and I don't want to look at them."

"Why?"

" 'Cos they look unhappy, *that's* why."

"I quite agree," said Lucy firmly. "Perhaps the sensible thing would be to find your protector and ask him to take you to see the crown jewels. Would you like that?"

"Better 'n this," said the boy laconically.

A beefeater came marching along and then stopped at the sight of them. "Here, young shaver," he exclaimed, "His Grace has nearly turned the whole guard out to look for you."

And then behind the beefeater came none other

than the Duke of Wardshire. Lucy involuntarily stepped back a pace, a hand flying to her mouth. His handsome face was as satanic-looking as she remembered, framed by the glossy black wings of his hair. He gave her a brief nod, not appearing to recognize her. He loomed over the small boy. "Where have you been, Peregrine?" he demanded wrathfully.

Lucy found her voice. "So *you* are Old Grizzly Face!"

The pale silver eyes surveyed her. "I beg your pardon, miss. Come, Peregrine."

"She don't like the beasts either," whined Peregrine. "She says we ought to see the crown jewels."

"And I say you deserve a whipping," said the duke wrathfully.

All the horrible tales she had heard about him rushed into Lucy's mind and she cried, "He is only a little boy, Your Grace, and the animals are not pleasant to watch, all dusty and dirty as they are."

He stood very still, his thin black eyebrows rising in surprise. "Well, well," he said softly. "Miss Lucy Bliss."

Lucy dropped a curtsy. "Your servant, Your Grace."

She felt awkward and ill at ease. Perhaps this child was one of the wicked duke's by-blows, for she could not imagine him taking the time to visit unfashionable sights with any child other than one of his own.

"Come along, Peregrine," snapped the duke.

But Peregrine felt he had found a more interesting protector. One small, chubby hand reached out and caught Lucy's. "Wanna stay with her," he said. He screwed up his eyes and opened his mouth. The duke wearily recognized the preparations. Peregrine was about to make a scene.

"But if you blubber," he said quickly, "you will be taken straight home and you will not see the crown jewels."

Peregrine's face uncreased, but he still clutched Lucy's hand tightly. "With her?" he demanded.

"Her name is Miss Lucy Bliss, and I am sure Miss Bliss does not want to be saddled with a whining brat." Peregrine's face began to fold up again and Lucy said, "I was going to see the jewels in any case. Come along, Peregrine, but you really must not cry to get what you want, you know. The Tower is full of brave soldiers, and what on earth will they think of you? Why, they will think, that is not a boy at all, but a *girl*."

Peregrine threw her a horrified look and then squared his small shoulders, released her hand, and strutted ahead with what he obviously thought was a martial air. The duke looked amused. He held out his arm to Lucy. "Shall we accompany the brat, Miss Bliss? We do not want him to run away again."

Lucy gingerly placed her hand on his arm and they moved ahead, Feathers and the footman following on behind. "Is . . . is Peregrine *yours*?" whispered Lucy.

"No, Miss Bliss. As far as I am aware, I do not have children. What a naughty mind you do have! Fie, for shame. Do you remember Mr. Rufus Graham?"

Lucy nodded.

"Peregrine is his godson. In a weak moment I offered to entertain him and have been regretting it bitterly ever since. Do you usually ask gentlemen about their by-blows?"

Lucy stumbled in her embarrassment, and he put a strong arm about her waist to support her, and the feel of that arm caused all sorts of new and strange sensations in her body. She quickly disengaged herself as Peregrine shouted, "Hurry up!"

Peregrine was enchanted by the jewels, and Lucy, watching the duke holding the boy up to get a better view, wondered at his tolerance, for she was beginning to understand that Peregrine was sadly spoilt.

They then went together out into the sunshine. "Wannanice," said Peregrine, dancing up and down.

"What did he say?" asked Lucy.

"Translated," said the duke, "it means he wants an ice. No, Peregrine. Home."

The child turned quite purple in the face with rage, and Lucy stared in amazement as Peregrine leapt up and down and shrieked in a piercing voice.

"Stop!" shouted Lucy. "Just stop this minute, young man. You are a disgrace to the gentlemen of England. Look at the soldiers laughing at you. There is nothing more tedious than the tantrums of a spoilt brat. Stop it, I say."

Peregrine stopped in midshriek and stood looking up at her in comical bewilderment. "Much better," said Lucy. "Now you will go home quietly to your mama, and you will behave yourself. Do you understand me?"

Peregrine hung his head, and his straw topper fell off, revealing a thatch of auburn curls. Lucy retrieved the topper and put it firmly on his head. "Now, quick march."

"I am deeply indebted to you," said the duke with a smile that seemed to turn Lucy's bones to water. "Perhaps we shall meet again."

"That I doubt very much," said Lucy. "Good day to you. Come, Feathers; come, John."

The duke watched her walk away and experienced a tinge of regret. Lucy was wearing a simple morning gown, high at the neck and with long sleeves. On her head was a wide-brimmed hat, untrimmed, shadowing her face. She moved lightly and with grace. He felt a pang of pity for her, quickly dismissed. The resolute Lucy Bliss, he thought, was in her way more than a match for her mother.

Peregrine, unusually subdued, clutched the duke's hand as they walked into the main courtyard. Miss Lucy Bliss was standing by her carriage addressing her two servants, and her voice reached the duke's ears very clearly.

"Now, remember," Lucy was saying severely, "we did not meet the Duke of Wardshire, for if Mama knew of the encounter, she would use it to try to coerce him into calling. Think what a disaster for poor Belinda if he married her! With any luck, we will never see him again. In fact, I hope *I* never see him again."

Oh, she does, does she? thought the duke crossly. He thought about that remark as he delivered Peregrine home. He thought about it as he walked to his club. And then he decided that Miss Lucy Bliss needed to be taught a lesson. He would call once, just for the sheer hell of irritating her, and would appear interested in Belinda. Then let Lucy Bliss try to cope with that!

* * *

Mrs. Bliss was in high alt. She had secured vouchers for Almack's Assembly Rooms for both daughters. This she had done by calling on one of the formidable patronesses, Mrs. Drummond Burrell, when that lady had the headache. Mrs. Bliss was unsnubbable. She had talked and talked, saying there was no need to send the vouchers through the post, she would just take them with her, and the patroness ended up giving them to her, just to get rid of that hammering voice.

Society soon got to hear of Mrs. Bliss's triumph and could hardly believe it. But through the grapevine they knew the duke was in town and had not called on the Bliss household. And had not Mrs. Tommy Watkins heard Mr. Rufus Graham talk about Mrs. Bliss's visit to Sarsey, and had he not said that the duke had been horrified by Mrs. Bliss? So, stunned as they were by Mrs. Bliss's success with the Almack's vouchers, they nonetheless waited gleefully for her downfall.

The fact that the duke was in town and had not called was beginning to irritate Mrs. Bliss, although she did not discuss the matter with her daughters. She sent the duke letters telling him that Belinda was pining for him; she sent him presents of hothouse grapes and chocolates, just as if he were ill, and the duke sent them back. The first ball of the Season was looming perilously close. It was at Lord Harby's in St. James's Square. Everyone knew Wardshire had accepted an invitation to that ball. Mrs. Bliss knew her hopes would be ruined if he cut her in front of everyone.

She was just wondering whether to manufacture an illness to prevent her going when her butler came in with an embossed card on a silver tray.

Mrs. Bliss picked it up wearily. She was starting to say crossly that she was not up to seeing anyone when the Duke of Wardshire's name in curly script seemed to shriek up at her. She clutched her heart and gasped. "Oh, my stars! Fan me, ye winds! Belinda! Get Feathers. Finest gown. Pink sprig with the four flounces. Quick! Quick! Show His Grace up."

As the duke was standing patiently in the hall and listening with an amused ear to all the frantic bustle abovestairs, a small gray man emerged from a room leading onto the hall and gave him a bow.

"Mr. Bliss at your service," said the gray man.

"And Wardshire, at yours," said the duke, returning the bow.

"Wardshire!" exclaimed Mr. Bliss in ludicrous dismay. "Oh, dear! Oh, dear!" He backed into the room whence he had come, and then there was a click as Mr. Bliss locked himself in.

The butler appeared, and the duke followed him upstairs to a drawing room on the first floor. He was served with wine and told that the ladies would join him presently. So the duke sipped his wine and listened with relish to the continuing sounds of panic which were filtering down from abovestairs.

At last Mrs. Bliss appeared, shepherding Belinda before her. Behind them came Lucy, her wide eyes meeting those of the duke with a message of appeal. He knew she did not want him to mention that meeting at the Tower, and fought down a malicious desire not to oblige her.

"Your Grace!" Mrs. Bliss advanced on him as he rose to his feet. "We are honored. Girls. Make your curtsies."

"I heard you were in London," said the duke

smoothly, "and am come to pay my respects," just as if he had never received any of those gifts or letters from Mrs. Bliss.

"Charmed," fluttered Mrs. Bliss. "Belinda, do but fetch your portfolio of watercolors to show His Grace."

Belinda found her voice. "I am not the artist of the family. Lucy is."

"Such modesty!" trilled Mrs. Bliss. The duke eyed Belinda speculatively as she went to fetch her portfolio. She was indeed a vastly pretty girl and appeared to have a sweet nature. But even with a more bearable mother, he could not consider her as a possible bride. She was barely out of the schoolroom. As Mrs. Bliss talked on, about the weather, about fashions, and about social tittle-tattle, he turned his attention to Lucy. She had not curled her hair the night before and it was almost straight, fine as a baby's, silver-fair, giving her an elfin appearance. He found himself intrigued by the strength of character he suspected lay under that fey exterior. Belinda shyly brought forward her drawings. He glanced through them. They were neat watercolors, fairly well executed, nothing out of the common way. But he praised them lavishly, feeling that if he did not, then Mrs. Bliss might make her younger daughter's life a misery by inflicting long and tedious art lessons on her. Belinda thanked him and took the portfolio away and then came back with another. "These are Lucy's," she said. "I think them very fine."

Ignoring Mrs. Bliss's protests that he could not possibly want to see Lucy's "little scribblings," the duke opened the portfolio. They were very good indeed and not at all like the drawings and watercolors of a young society lady. At the top were a few conventional watercolors that he immediately felt sure Lucy had done to please her mother. Underneath them he came across some powerful sketches in India ink: an ostler flirting with a serving girl, a child with a hoop, an old beggar, and at the bottom, one that made him draw in a sharp breath. "I will take this to the light," he said, and walked over to the window while Lucy, flushed and miserable, stared after him in an agony of embarrassment.

The picture portrayed Belinda holding hands with the Duke of Wardshire. Tears were running down Belinda's half-averted face. The duke, although correct in morning dress, sported a neat pair of horns and a tail. Before them stood a large and triumphant Mrs. Bliss, her chubby arms raised in a blessing. Behind the duke and Belinda stood Mr. Bliss, reading a book. It was captioned: "A Mother's Blessing."

The duke swung round. Lucy clasped her hands in supplication, her large eyes wide with fright.

"You seem vastly interested in that picture of Lucy's," said Mrs. Bliss. "Let me see it, Your Grace."

" 'Tis nothing but a little watercolor, but it pleases me," said the duke. He rolled it up. "May I have it, Miss Bliss?"

"By all means," said Lucy faintly, frightened to protest.

"Well, there's no denying Lucy is the clever one of the family," said Mrs. Bliss. "Too much intelligence by half. A sad disadvantage, and the gentlemen never like it. Will you be at the Harbys' ball?"

"Yes," said the duke.

"How nice for Belinda," commented Mrs. Bliss complacently.

He wished he had not come. He bowed slightly without replying and made toward the door.

"Never say you are leaving us so soon!" Mrs. Bliss almost looked as if she were going to bar his way.

"I am afraid I must."

'Then we shall see you at the ball. Belinda dances like an angel." Again that brief bow and then he was gone.

He was angry, thought Lucy. He'll never forgive me. She wanted to shout at Belinda for having shown her paintings, but poor Belinda had not seen that last painting, so she could hardly be blamed.

When she finally managed to speak to Belinda alone, Belinda listened to Lucy tell of that picture and then began to giggle helplessly.

"It is not *funny*," said Lucy. "He was *furious*. Mark my words, he took it away so that he could destroy it at the first opportunity. Why are you laughing?"

"Don't you see?" Belinda mopped her eyes. "I was quite cast down when I heard he had called, for I feared he might want me after all. But now he has seen my dear sister's portrayal of him as the devil, he will have nothing more to do with either of us."

Lucy gave a reluctant grin. "Why is it you, the younger sister, have such common sense? You have the right of it. Good-bye forever, dear Duke of Wardshire!"

"You *what*?" exclaimed Mr. Graham.

The duke stretched out his long legs toward the fire. "You heard. I called on La Bliss."

"What were you about to encourage that pretentious mushroom?"

"A whim, and I was well punished for it."

"I am sure you were. Did she deafen you with her vulgar, hectoring voice?"

"I expected that. No, it was not that, dear Rufus, which was the punishment. Rather it was the artistic efforts of Miss Lucy Bliss."

"The plain one."

"I would hardly describe her as plain. Her looks are less obvious than those of her sister." He reached down beside his chair and lifted up Lucy's drawing, carefully unrolled it, and handed it to Mr. Graham.

"The minx!" he gasped. "But you must admit it is very good. She has you to the life."

"Complete with horns and tail?"

"You can hardly blame her for that," said Mr. Graham reasonably. "After all, you have spent years in fostering your vile reputation. What are you going to do with it? Burn it?"

The duke took the drawing from him and looked down at it thoughtfully. "I think I shall frame it. It amuses me."

"There's one thing for sure," said Mr. Graham. "The Bliss girls don't want you. A new experience for you." He gave a little cough and, throwing the duke a sideways look, said airily, "You will never guess who I met in the park."

"Now, how could I? I cannot read minds."

"Lady Fortescue."

The duke rolled up Lucy's drawing with careful fingers.

"Indeed," he said in a colorless voice.

"Yes, indeed, and she asked after you most particularly."

"I am sure she did," said the duke dryly. "Dukes are very interesting people, are they not? Much more interesting than mere army captains."

"Meaning had you been a duke at the time you proposed, she would have accepted you?"

"Of course."

"You may be wrong. Look at the Bliss sisters."

"No, you may look at the Bliss sisters if you wish. I have done more than enough to encourage the horrible Mrs. Bliss. I intend to give her the cut direct at Harby's ball."

"Hardly fair." Mr. Graham pursed his lips. "I mean it's all your own fault for encouraging the woman in the first place. Don't dance with her girls. Give her a common nod; that will be enough. Now I must go. A pressing game of cards awaits me."

When his friend had left, the duke sat for a few moments. Then he rose and collected his hat and stick from the hall and made his way out to make a call. He did not need to ask where she lived. He had found that out as soon as he had reached London.

He marched up the steps of a slim town house in Manchester Square and knocked at the door and then presented his card to the butler, who retreated up the stairs with it, telling him to wait. The duke wondered what she would look like after all these years. The butler came hurrying back. "Pray follow me, Your Grace. Lady Fortescue will be delighted to receive you."

He mounted the narrow staircase and then paused at the entrance to the drawing room. Clarinda Fortescue ran to meet him, both hands outstretched. His kissed both her hands and allowed her to lead him to a sofa in front of the fire. She had not changed, he thought bleakly. Her hair was still as black and glossy as his own. Her eyes, Slav eyes, he used to call them, were as blue as ever, with that intriguing black ring around the iris. Her figure was a trifle fuller, but she was elegantly gowned, and the whiteness of her skin did not even betray one wrinkle.

He leaned back slightly and surveyed her. "So," he said, "you decided not to wait for me."

"I tried so hard to," she said in a low voice. "Oh, if only you knew. But Papa and Mama were so stern. They *forced* me to marry Fortescue."

He fought against the old spell of her attraction. He remembered her parents, Mr. and Mrs. Bellingham, as rather a quiet, timid couple who let their beautiful daughter do pretty much what she wanted. But what *he* wanted now, he realized, was revenge. He intended to make Clarinda fall in love with him and pay her back for some of the pain she had caused him.

"And was your marriage not happy?"

She took out a little wisp of lace-edged cambric and dabbed her eyes. "I was so unhappy," she whispered. "All the time, I thought of you."

He took her hand and smiled down at her. "Well, I am back and we are both free. Do you go to Harby's ball?"

"Oh, yes. Will you dance with me?"

"Of course. I shall be the most envied man there."

She gave him a glinting sideways glance and murmured, "All the gossips will have it that you are set on courting some provincial chit just out of the schoolroom."

"I assume by that they mean Belinda Bliss. No, my dear, much too young for me. But I must not stay long. Your reputation . . ."

"My reputation will not be harmed," she said. "All must know how I have pined for you."

She modestly bent her head and so escaped seeing the flash of cynicism in the duke's eyes.

"Nonetheless, we must not give the gossips any fuel." He released her hand, rose, and bowed before her.

"When will I see you again?" she asked.

"At the Harbys' ball."

She pouted. "Not before then?"

"I am afraid I have much to attend to. But I shall count the hours."

He felt slightly ashamed of himself as he walked away. It was all such an easy game when one was a duke. Except if your name happens to be Lucy Bliss, mocked a voice in his head, and he strode off round the square as if to walk away from it.

As soon as he had disappeared around the corner of the square, Lady Fortescue turned from the window and ran to a looking glass and patted her curls. "I shall have him," she told her reflection. "I shall be a duchess!"

How fortunate it had been, she thought, that old Lord Fortescue had died so conveniently. Now she was free. She dimly remembered her parents' protests when she had announced she meant to marry that elderly lord. But Fortescue had been rich and he had a title, and she had had a mind to be "my lady." But she had worked for it. What a dismal old satyr he had turned out to be. But she brightened; the duke was a virile, handsome man, much more handsome than the young captain she had turned down all those years ago. Besides, his wickedness was exciting. Lady Fortescue then went to her bedchamber and summoned her maid. There was no time to have a new ballgown made. But what she chose from what she had must dazzle the duke.

At supper that evening, Mrs. Bliss's voice rose and fell remorselessly as she regaled her husband with every bit of the duke's visit. "He even took away one of Lucy's little drawings, and do you know why he did that, Mr. Bliss?"

"Because she is a very fine artist," suggested her husband.

"No, no! 'Tis because *Belinda* said Lucy was a good artist, and it was obvious to me that he would do anything to please our Belinda."

"Except dance with her at the Harbys' ball," put in Lucy.

Mrs. Bliss looked at her in amazement. "I beg your pardon!"

"You suggested he would dance with Belinda, or that was what you meant," said Lucy patiently, "and he would not be drawn. I think he called out of mischief. All society knows you have been bragging about your visit to the duke's home. *I* feel he was maliciously raising your hopes just in order to snub you before everyone at Lord Harby's."

"And I think you have been addling your brains with too many novels."

Mr. Bliss found his voice. It was a dry and dusty voice, as if it did not get much use. "You must remember, my dear," he said, "that Wardshire does have a vile reputation."

"Pooh!" Mrs. Bliss snapped her chubby fingers in

disdain. "He is a fine man and will make Belinda an excellent husband."

"And what has Belinda to say to that?" asked Mr. Bliss.

Mrs. Bliss looked at him with the same astonished expression that might have crossed her face had the fire irons decided to ask a question.

"Belinda is too young to know her own mind," she said firmly. "She will be guided by me!"

Chapter Three

FOG.

Who in society could ever have believed that the Almighty would have allowed fog to descend on London on the day of Lord Harby's ball?

Lucy, used to the gentle white mists of the country, was fascinated. Mrs. Bliss was occupied in overseeing the dressmaker who had called to make some last-minute alterations to Belinda's gown, so Lucy persuaded Feathers to go out walking with her.

Everywhere fog gripped the throat and set the eyes watering. Linkboys scurried past, their lights little bobbing sequins in the Stygian gloom. Street traders had become bloodcurdling monsters, misshapen black bundles looming out of the darkness and shrieking their wares. London had been turned into a city of ghosts.

A fop with a painted face appeared in front of Lucy with the startling suddenness of an apparition and then was gone.

In Oxford Street two carriages had locked wheels. Fifty grim and muffled ghosts stood about, watching the battling drivers trying to free themselves. Farther on, crossing the road, a monster with two yellow eyes bore down on Lucy, who let out a yelp of fright until she realized she was looking at an approaching carriage. In Hanover Square, men were putting down cobbles on a tarry base. Except they were no longer men. The thick fog turned them into demons pushing flaming caldrons of tar about. A flurry of wind blew the flames this way and that, lighting up the faces of the men, glittering on their belt buckles and turning their bare arms red.

Lucy was enchanted. She wished Belinda were with her. How could Belinda be so . . . stoic, Belinda, who endured pinnings and fittings and her mother's voice without a murmur of complaint. I hope she gets a man worthy of her, thought Lucy suddenly. Not Wardshire. He belongs in this setting, where the whole of London has been transformed into the pit. "I say, Feathers," she said aloud, "surely no one will hold a ball in such weather. The fog has entered the houses. We shall barely be able to see our partners."

"Don't see as how it can be canceled," said Feathers practically. "Can't manage to tell everyone not to come."

"But surely a great deal of them *won't* come," said Lucy eagerly, "and it will not be nearly so terrifying an occasion."

"I hear a lot of servants' gossip," said Feathers, "and believe me, miss, they would walk through fire and water this night to get a look at the wicked duke. Now we'd best be getting back. Madam will be shouting for me."

They were met in the hall by a furious Mrs. Bliss. "How could you go out on such a day, Lucy? Look at your hair! Look at your clothes! Filthy. Feathers, you should have had more sense. Go to Miss Belinda immediately. She needs you. Lucy, I do not approve of baths except in dire circumstances, and this is one of them. John," she said, turning to a footman, "carry the bath up to Miss Lucy's bedchamber."

Lucy made for the stairs and Mrs. Bliss followed, her voice loud with complaint.

At last Lucy was able to sink into a rose-scented bath in front of her bedroom fire and listen to her mother's voice, muted by distance as it sounded faintly from Belinda's room. After she had finished her bath, Lucy ordered more cans of hot water and washed her hair thoroughly, something she knew would have shocked her mother could she have seen it. Washing one's whole head was regarded as a dangerous practice, leading to toothache at the least, and at the worst, dampness of the brain.

Feathers appeared two hours later complaining that her own clothes had been ruined by the fog and she did not know how she was ever going to get them clean. Lucy stood obediently while Feathers dressed her. She had little interest in her own appearance. This was to be Belinda's coming-out, not her own.

Her gown was of white muslin but threaded with silver at the neck and hem. A small coronet of silver roses with silver leaves was placed on her hair. "Hope that dressmaker knows what he's about," grumbled Feathers. "You don't look . . . well, bless me, you don't look like the other young ladies are going to look."

"I am sure you are wrong," said Lucy calmly. "I am wearing white muslin. Very correct."

There was a scratching at the door and then the dressmaker, Monsieur Farré, entered. He walked slowly around Lucy. "Something else," he murmured. "I have it." He darted out and was shortly back, bearing a box of silver sequins and silver thread. He deftly stitched sequins here and there among the silver roses and leaves of Lucy's coronet. At last he drew back, satisfied. "You look like the frost fairy," he said with satisfaction.

Lucy laughed. "I declare you are a success due as much to your clever compliments as to your art with the needle."

When both Feathers and the dressmaker had gone, Lucy thought about that compliment. Frost fairy. She had a longing to run to the long glass and look at herself properly for the first time. But how much better, she reflected, not to look, to *imagine* herself beautiful for just one whole glorious evening.

Belinda came in to join her, and Lucy was immediately glad she had not studied her own reflection. Belinda was a picture in rose muslin. She had a Juliet cap made of tiny roses on her glossy pomaded curls. Her small and pretty mouth had been delicately rouged. The whiteness of her excellent bosom swelled above the low neck of her gown. She looked like a Meissen figure, thought Lucy, perfect in every detail, full of color, while she herself felt like a wraith in comparison.

"How beautiful you look, Lucy," said Belinda in awe. "It is the very first time I have ever seen you look beautiful."

Lucy felt a rush of excitement. Belinda in her quiet way always spoke her mind. "I have not really dared to look properly," she said with a laugh.

"Then go to the glass," urged Belinda. "Look now."

Lucy approached the long glass cautiously. Bands

of fog lay across the room, and her reflection appeared to waver in the candlelight. Her large gray eyes stared back at her; the fine white and silver muslin appeared to float about her slim body, and the candlelight sparked silver lights from the sequins in her headdress. And then Belinda's reflection appeared behind her. Belinda glowing in rose pink. I am part of this fog, thought Lucy. Insubstantial. She wished she had not looked at herself, but comforted herself with the thought that this was Belinda's great evening.

As the hour to leave approached, even the usually calm Belinda became nervous. "What if they all cut us to teach Mama a lesson?" she worried.

"They may plan to," said Lucy, "but one look at you and the men will crowd around you. For me it will be different. If only one were allowed to take a book along."

They fell silent until Belinda threw an anguished look at the clock and exclaimed, "We should be on our way. Ring the bell, Lucy dear." Feathers answered the summons, rustling in wearing her best black silk.

"Where is Mama?" demanded Lucy.

"Resting in her room."

"But does she not realize the time?"

"I believe Mrs. Bliss wishes to make an entrance."

"Oh, she *would*," said Lucy crossly. "Mind you, all she is doing is making sure that she will be snubbed as publicly as possible."

It was another hour before Mrs. Bliss, resplendent in gold taffeta, bustled in and commanded them to make themselves ready. "We may leave," she said, "for Wardshire will have made his entrance by now. We could not go before, because everyone is waiting to see him and would not have time to concentrate on us."

It was then that the maid, Feathers, chose to drop her bombshell. "Lady Fortescue will be there, madam."

"Who? And what is Lady Fortescue to me?"

"Lady Fortescue was Clarinda Bellingham."

"And?"

"The Duke of Wardshire proposed to her when he was an army captain. She said she would wait for him but went off and married Lord Fortescue, old enough to be her grandfather. 'Tis said the duke never got over it."

"Well, well, so she is married."

"She is a widow, and her maid told Lady Jessy's maid who told Mrs. Hardcastle's maid who told me that he had called on her at her town house in Manchester Square, and on the very day he called here. She peeped round the door and he was holding her hand. Lady Fortescue is now putting it about that marriage to the duke is in the offing."

Lucy felt sorry for her mother. Mrs. Bliss looked shattered. Then she rallied. "He was calling on an old friend, that is all. I am persuaded of it. Just look at Belinda. He will not have eyes this night for any other." And so she talked on and on until she had talked herself back into a good humor. Mrs. Bliss was her own best friend, and she herself was the only person she ever really listened to.

Hoarfrost was glittering on the streets as they stepped out into the fog, all carefully wrapped like packages to keep their gowns from getting dirty.

Lucy began to feel tremendously excited. She was young and she was going to her first London ball.

Their carriage inched its way through the gloom. For once, Mrs. Bliss fell silent. Opposite her sat Mr. Bliss, uncomfortable in his evening clothes and high, starched cravat behind which his face, seen fitfully in the swinging carriage lamp, looked miserably at the world like a small gray animal peering over a snowdrift. He obviously longed to be back with his beloved books and out of the naughty world of society.

They all alighted at Lord Harby's house and walked up the red carpet to the door past a double guard of liveried footmen. From the ballroom at the back of the house came the sweet sound of a waltz. In the room set aside for the ladies, Feathers unwrapped them from their cloaks and calashes and fussed over them. Lucy was the first to join her father in the hall.

He gave her a startled look and raised his quizzing glass. "I' faith, Lucy," he said, "you are quite beautiful."

Lucy felt a warm glow spreading inside her, and when they were joined by Mrs. Bliss and Belinda, she walked almost jauntily up the stairs.

She heard her mother's cluck of dismay. Mrs. Bliss had mistimed their entrance. Lord and Lady Harby were not waiting to receive them. They had joined their guests, and when they entered the ballroom, they were faced with a crowd of backs.

"This will never do," said Mrs. Bliss, and then, like the Grand Old Duke of York, she marched them down again.

"Now what?" asked Lucy impatiently. She had been all set to enter that dreadful ballroom buoyed up by her father's compliment, but her mother's action had given her time to reflect, time to think sadly that her father had been trying to be kind.

"What is the point of squeezing in now?" demanded Mrs. Bliss. "We will wait until this dance is finished."

And so they waited . . . and waited . . . for it was a country dance which lasted quite half an hour.

"Now!" said Mrs. Bliss as the music died away, and up they went again.

They hesitated on the threshold, and society turned and stared while Mrs. Bliss edged Belinda forward and visibly preened.

Lucy was to learn that society always stared openly. Hard eyes looked at them through quizzing glasses and over fans. One lady near them said loudly, " 'Tis that Bliss creature," and turned away.

Mr. Bliss, for once in his life, took over. He appeared to be angry. Deaf to his wife's protests, he ushered the girls across the floor and found them seats.

"I wouldn't have recognized the older one," said Mr. Graham. "Your artist. Out of the common way. I am glad the father has found them places to sit down, because the buzz has it that no one is going to dance with the Bliss girls because the pushing mama has put everyone's back up."

The duke studied them. Belinda was looking enchanting, he thought, fresh and lovely and endearing. Lucy was leaning protectively toward her. He then looked round the room and caught the eye of Lady Fortescue. She gave him a slow, seductive smile over her fan and waited expectantly, obviously expecting him to join her.

But he was all at once sorry for the Bliss girls. It was their first London ball.

"I think we should ask them to dance," he said to Mr. Graham. "I do not like being dictated to by society."

"But you'll never get that mother off your neck," expostulated Mr. Graham. "Everyone is waiting to see who you lead to the floor. If you take up one of her girls before anyone else, it will go to Mrs. Bliss's head and she'll have you in church before you know what has happened. Oh, well, I see by that martial light in your eye that you are determined. The next dance is the quadrille. I'll take up the fair Belinda and leave you with your artist."

"No," said the duke. "I'll take Belinda. I bring out the worst in Miss Bliss, and she should be on her best behavior this evening."

Mr. Graham was uneasily aware of all eyes watching them as they made their way toward the Bliss family. The duke courteously introduced him to Mr. Bliss. He asked Lucy to dance while the duke asked Belinda.

As they led their partners to a set, the duke noticed the fury on Lady Fortescue's face. Why! I am having my revenge without even having to court her, he thought, and set himself to be particularly kind to Belinda. She was an artless creature, he thought, good-natured and quite unspoilt. He wondered what Lucy was saying to Mr. Graham, for Mr. Graham was looking amused.

"Why on earth did you do it?" Lucy was asking.

"Do what?" asked Mr. Graham innocently.

"Why, ask us to dance, of course."

"Why not?" countered Mr. Graham gallantly. "You are the prettiest girls in the room."

"Pooh! I trust *you*, sir, but I fear your friend

means mischief. What he thinks of Mama is easy to guess."

Mr. Graham laughed. "Are you always so forthright?"

Lucy wrinkled her brow while he watched her with some amusement. "Yes, I think I am," she said at last. "I think it comes from being plain. One does not expect compliments of any kind, and when one receives them, well, one simply does not believe a word of it."

"We are about to begin," he said. "I trust you know the steps. It is a difficult dance."

"Oh, Belinda and I dance *very* well," remarked Lucy.

And so they did, thought Mr. Graham with some amazement as the dance progressed. Lucy was particularly good, light and graceful. He found he was proud of being her partner. He reflected that he liked her honest manner. The duke had made sure that the Bliss girls would be a success that evening. But he found he wanted some more of Lucy's company.

When the dance finished, he bowed low before her and begged her to let him have the supper dance. "Now, that *is* kind of you," said Lucy, "for I am very hungry and I feared if no one asked me, that I might have to sit with Mama and *starve*, for she would be so piqued, she would not move at all."

"So how did you fare?" asked the duke when he had delivered Belinda to her mother.

"Very well," said Mr. Graham. "Miss Bliss dances like an angel. In fact, I have the honor of taking her in to supper."

The duke felt a twinge of annoyance. "There is no need to go *that* far, Rufus."

"I asked her to please myself, I assure you. Oh, it is the waltz and there is Lady Fortescue, obviously looking for you. She is coming toward us."

"I wonder if Miss Bliss dances the waltz as well as she does the quadrille," said the duke, and before Lady Fortescue could reach them, he approached the Bliss family again. Mr. Graham, not wanting to be left with Lady Fortescue, hurriedly followed him, and while the duke asked Lucy to dance, he asked Belinda.

The gentlemen at the ball who had planned to hold themselves aloof from the Bliss family watched in amazement. Mr. Anstruther turned to a friend and said, "But we were all told that Mrs. Bliss is so awful that no one would dance with her girls, and yet Wardshire chooses to dance with them, and for a second time, too."

"Well," remarked his friend, Mr. Joseph Messenger, "you must admit the younger one is beautiful beyond compare. Family is well-to-do, ain't they? You can snub 'em if you like, but I'm going to have a dance with that dazzler as soon as I can."

The duke looked down at Lucy as she twirled under his arm. The thin silver muslin floated about her body. She obviously enjoyed dancing, so much, he thought a little crossly, that she had almost forgotten with whom she was dancing.

But Lucy was desperately aware of him, aware of the feel of his strong hand at her waist. That touch of his caused all sorts of suffocating emotions in her body, emotions she had not known she had, and she thought he must be truly evil. As they danced together and wound around each other in the intricate steps, he was conscious of the grace and beauty of her body, of her slim hips and small, high breasts.

Plumpness was all the rage, but he found Lucy's beauty more appealing. And she did have a kind of beauty, he thought. Not fashionable, but with her wide, expressive gray eyes and baby-fine hair, infinitely appealing.

Speculative eyes and jealous eyes watched them. The duke in black evening coat and black pantaloons so tight, they looked painted on his long, muscular legs, and the girl in silver and white. Lady Fortescue, dancing with a general, contrived to keep the couple in sight. What was Wardshire about to encourage the social pretentions of that dreadful family?

And the duke had done his work well, for no sooner was the waltz over than both the Bliss girls were besieged by partners.

Lady Fortescue found the duke at her elbow and said, "Chasing children, Wardshire? The pretty one is surely only seventeen, and the elder, about nineteen."

"And both very pretty," he said. "Shall we dance?"

She smiled at him. "I thought you meant to cut me."

"Never," he said. "You are the most beautiful woman here, and none can hold a candle to you."

Lucy, dancing with the energetic Mr. Anstruther, reflected dully that the duke and Lady Fortescue—for she had made a point of asking who the lady was—were very well suited, the duke with his harsh, demonic looks, and Lady Fortescue with her overblown beauty.

At least, thought Lucy, Belinda is safe.

But it transpired that the duke had asked Belinda for the supper dance, and so Lucy, sitting next to them at a long table with Mr. Graham, had leisure to notice the way the duke was expertly teasing Belinda and flirting with her. And Mr. Graham noticed that the duke was flirting with Belinda while casting sidelong looks along the table at Lucy to see how she was taking it.

That drawing of Lucy's must really have irritated Wardshire, he thought.

As supper drew to a close, Mr. Graham noticed Mr. Bliss rising to leave the room, and Lady Fortescue going up to his wife. Lady Fortescue was fanning herself slowly and talking to Mrs. Bliss, and Mrs. Bliss was puffing herself up in the pouter pigeon way she did when she was angry.

The rest of the ball passed in an exhausting whirl for Lucy and Belinda, and it was five in the morning before they made their way home.

"Well, that went very well," said Mrs. Bliss complacently. "Mind you, I confess I was thrown when that Fortescue creature had the temerity to tell me she was as good as affianced to Wardshire, but he only danced the one dance with her and did not take *her* in to supper."

"I think," said Belinda cautiously, "that the duke favored us because, Mama, society was determined to cut us, and he is a contrary sort of person."

"Fiddlesticks!" said her mother.

Mr. Bliss spoke suddenly. "There is his reputation to consider, Mrs. Bliss. Such a dissipated rake often finds the idea of corrupting the young titillating."

"He cannot have a bad reputation!" exclaimed Mrs. Bliss. "He is a duke!"

And as far as she was concerned, that settled the matter. Her busy mind turned to what the girls should wear at Almack's opening subscription ball, and they arrived at the house with her voice remorselessly beating on their ears as she discussed muslins and taffetas, ribbons and silks. There was no respite when they were indoors, for she roused the servants and ordered the tea tray so that she could further turn over the triumphs of the night and plan gowns to wear to Almack's.

Feeling mentally bruised and battered, Belinda and Lucy finally crept up to bed. "Come into my room, Belinda," urged Lucy. "I want to talk to you about the duke."

"You, too," sighed Belinda. "All Mama does when she is not going on like a haberdasher is to talk about the duke." She plunked herself down on Lucy's bed and yawned.

"If he asked you to marry him, you would not accept him, would you?" asked Lucy.

"I might,' said Belinda. "I have to marry someone, you know, and he does seem kind."

"Think of his reputation!"

"I think perhaps all the stories about him are made up," said Belinda cautiously. "In fact, it would not surprise me at all if he were really something of a puritan."

"You are such a kind innocent," said Lucy fondly, "that you think everyone is the same. It is a good thing I am here to protect you. But *I* have a beau! Mr. Graham asked Mama if he could take me driving tomorrow. Today!" she corrected as a shaft of dawn sunlight crept between a chink in the shutters.

"Then if you approve of Mr. Graham," pointed out Belinda, "you must approve of the duke, for they are the best of friends, and I think Mr. Graham a very fine man."

"You do? Then come driving with us!"

"Not I. It was you he asked. I shall sleep all day long if Mama will let me. Why do you not ask Mr. Graham about the duke's black reputation? If anyone knows the truth, it is he."

"And if I were to find out that he is not so black as he has been painted, would you be interested in becoming his bride?"

"Perhaps. It would be a very fine thing to be a duchess."

"But what of love?"

Belinda giggled. "Silly! I am in London to find a husband, not to fall in love. That's what you do *after* marriage."

"Belinda! You shock me!"

"Lucy, sometimes I think you are the younger. You are so romantic. I do not really mind who I wed so long as he is kind and will take me somewhere far away from the sound of Mama's voice. I would have my own household, my own servants, my own—"

"Babies," said Lucy. "What of babies? One every nine months until you die young."

"Too many novels, Lucy, that's your problem. Whoever marries me will wait until I produce an heir or two and then take himself off to his club and his mistress. People do not live happily ever after."

Lucy looked distressed. "How did you come by such cynicism?"

"I watch. I look. I observe."

"But is there not something inside you that cries out that for you it will be different?"

"Of course," said the ever practical Belinda. "But I pay it no heed. I have one ambition in life, and that is to have my own home, and that's a very comfortable ambition to have. If I have any more days of Mama's voice, then I shall marry the very first man who asks me." She smiled slyly at her sister. "And that may be the duke . . . unless, of course, you want him for yourself."

"Don't be nonsensical!"

Belinda rose and gave her sister a hug. "Do not let your imagination play you tricks, Lucy. It will have you believing a saint a villain, and a villain a saint. And you must not fuss so about me. I am well able to take care of myself."

"Girls! Girls! Are you awake?" Mrs. Bliss's approaching voice.

Belinda ran from the room while Lucy tore off her headdress and, fully dressed, dived under the blankets and pulled them over her head.

A few moments later she heard her mother's voice quite close by. "Are you asleep?"

Lucy pretended to snore. "Tch!" said Mrs. Bliss. "Gone to sleep and left all the candles burning." She moved about, extinguishing them. She bent over the bed. "I was very proud of my girls tonight," she said. She drew the blankets gently down from Lucy's head and noticed she was lying in her ball gown. "Good heavens. She can't sleep like that." Mrs. Bliss rang the bell furiously until Feathers, cross and yawning and dressed in her nightgown, answered its summons.

"Just look at Lucy," cried Mrs. Bliss. "Gone to bed in her good ball gown. Rouse her this minute, Feathers, and get her washed and changed. I will stay here and keep her company."

Lucy reluctantly pretended to awake. Feathers fussed over her while Mrs. Bliss talked and talked as the sun rose higher outside and London came to life. When Lucy at last fell asleep, Mrs. Bliss was still sitting by the bed, talking and talking.

Chapter Four

THE NEXT DAY Lucy wondered for the hundredth time if her mother ever slept. Somewhere between dawn and the time when Lucy was to go out driving with Mr. Rufus Graham, Mrs. Bliss had contrived to find out all about that gentleman.

"Five thousand a year," she told Lucy, "and most of it in consuls. A tidy estate in the south of Scotland. Pity it's in Scotland, but he doesn't seem to spend much time there, and therefore neither will you. 'Twould amaze me if you were to wed before Belinda, but there it is. Don't go shaming me by giving Mr. Graham a disgust of you by making those outspoken remarks. Gentlemen like *silent* ladies."

"Indeed, Mama? Was that what attracted Papa to you?"

"We managed things better in our day," said Mrs. Bliss, unaware of the sarcasm in her daughter's voice. "His parents picked me out and approached my parents, and our lawyers settled the rest. So dignified. Remember to lower your eyes becomingly. Don't slouch. Sit bolt upright in his carriage and do not let your back touch the back of the carriage seat. Several gentlemen who danced with you and Belinda will call this afternoon or send cards.

Wardshire has already sent his card, which means he don't mean to call. Irritating man. Your hair looks too soft. Feathers, the curling tongs. It must curl under her bonnet."

A footman appeared in the doorway at that moment to say that Monsieur Farré had called for Belinda's latest fitting, and Mrs. Bliss hurried out.

"Oh, put the curling tongs away, Feathers," said Lucy wearily. "I really do not want to go out today. I want to sleep and sleep."

"It will only be for an hour at the most," said Feathers soothingly, "and Miss Belinda will take up most of Madam's time, for the milliner is to call later."

Lucy hoped her mother would be too busy to be present when Mr. Graham called to collect her, but Mrs. Bliss was there when he arrived, praising Lucy to the skies with all the fulsome compliments she usually reserved for Belinda.

Mr. Graham had an open carriage, because it would have been bad form to be closeted with an unchaperoned lady in a closed one. He was driving himself, with a tiger on the backstrap. The tiger was a small, evil-looking boy with a pinched white face, a wet mouth, and a knowing look. London, thought Lucy sadly, was full of such working children, children who had really never known the joys of childhood at all.

The carriage, a phaeton, was drawn by two splendid white horses, and Mr. Graham handled his whip like an expert. He pointed out various buildings and talked in a light, easy, and undemanding way. When they turned in at the park gates, Lucy decided to take Belinda's advice and ask Mr. Graham about the wicked duke.

"I have heard some shocking tales of the Duke of Wardshire," said Lucy, glancing nervously at the sky, which was becoming darker by the minute. She was enjoying this brief respite from her mother's voice and was not anxious to be driven back to the house too soon.

"Oh, yes?" Mr. Graham sounded cautious. The duke had left for his country estates that morning and had been strangely displeased when he had learned his friend was engaged to take Miss Lucy on a drive. His last words had been "I did wrong to encourage you to pay court to the Bliss girls. The mother is beyond the pale. Do what you can to depress their ambitions." Mr. Graham was sure that neither of the Bliss girls had any ambition to marry the duke, but he was growing increasingly fond of Lucy and did not want her to show any interest in Wardshire whatsoever, and had not Wardshire expressly told him to keep up the fiction of that black reputation?

"Are the stories about him true?" Lucy asked.

"I am afraid they are," said Mr. Graham solemnly.

"Then I am surprised you have such a friend!"

"I hope and pray he will settle down," said Mr. Graham.

"But surely some of the stories were exaggerated? I mean, black masses and things like that."

"I fear not, Miss Lucy. I could tell you . . . but I dare not!"

Her curiosity sharpened, Lucy said firmly, "You *must* tell me."

"The sad fact is that . . . Oh, I did so hope he had reformed!" Mr. Graham was beginning to enjoy himself. "But he has gone down to Sarsey for the express purpose of holding a black mass on Sunday in the family chapel. Of course, there was some hint of a human sacrifice, but *that*, I am persuaded, my dear Miss Lucy, is all a hum."

"This is dreadful!" Lucy's back was stiff with outrage, as straight and rigid as her mother could have wished. "To think we have had him in our home. To think I danced with him. He should be stopped!"

"Well, you know," said Mr. Graham amiably, "dukes are dukes. I mean, they've a lot of power and can do what they like."

"That is because no one ever dreams of reporting them to the authorities," exclaimed Lucy.

He shot her a nervous look. "I say, don't do anything silly."

"I have no intention of doing anything silly," said Lucy. "But Mama must be told or she will have Belinda married off to him."

"Don't think he wants Miss Belinda, and that's a fact," said Mr. Graham. "If you ask me, Lady Fortescue's the love of his life."

But this welcome piece of news, strangely enough, appeared to make Lucy angrier than ever.

Large, heavy drops of rain began to fall, and Mr. Graham turned smartly in the direction of home. But for once, Lucy could not wait to see her mother.

Mrs. Bliss listened aghast to Lucy's tale of the black mass and actually remained silent for two whole minutes after Lucy had finished speaking. Then she found her voice. "Fustian!" she said. "We have met Wardshire and he is a fine and noble gentleman." She took a deep breath and then went on and on until she had talked herself back into a comfortable state of mind.

Lucy escaped and went up to her room. Sunday

was only three days away. He must be exposed for the villain he was. But how to do it?

She thought hard and then hit on the idea of telling the *Morning Bugle*, a paper of radical traditions which delighted in exposing the sins and follies of the aristrocracy. Too determined to feel nervous about going out into London on her own, she made her escape while her mother was closeted with the milliner and hired a hack to take her to Fleet Street. At the offices of the *Morning Bugle*, she demanded haughtily to see the editor, and because of the richness of her clothes and the determination in her voice, she soon found herself in a small, inky cubbyhole which served the editor, Mr. Witherspoon, as an office.

He listened intently to her story and then said quietly that he would see what could be done. Lucy left, feeling a weight lifted off her mind. The newspaper would send someone to that black mass, and soon all London would read about it.

After she had gone, Mr. Witherspoon sat for some time in deep thought. He could not simply publish her story and perhaps risk a libel action from the duke. He eventually rose and put on his coat and made his way to Bow Street. He would tell the Runners and see what could be done. If the Runners decided to investigate, then it meant he could send along a reporter, and the reporter would have every reason to be there.

The magistrate at Bow Street listened uneasily to the editor's story. He felt he could not ignore it. All the social columns in the newspapers had already hinted at the duke's devilish goings-on down at Sarsey when it was known that Wardshire planned to attend his first Season.

"We must be there," he said. "Wardshire cannot blame us for checking if it should prove to be a hum. There are many dark stories about him circulating London."

Lucy, for her part, returned home and contrived to signal to Belinda that she wanted to see her alone. Mrs. Bliss took them that evening to a musicale, and after the concert when she was busy talking to the mothers of eligible sons, Lucy drew Belinda aside. "I must take this opportunity," she whispered, "to tell you what I have done."

She briefly outlined what Mr. Graham had said and her own visit to the newspaper office.

"Oh, dear," said Belinda when Lucy had finished. "This is all wrong. You know, Lucy, duke or no duke, if Wardshire had been up to any villainy, then he would have been arrested long before this. If he plans to hold a black mass in his private chapel, then that is his affair. But think, dear sister. Just think. We have met Wardshire. Can you imagine such a grand gentleman holding a black mass? He would find it all too undignified."

Lucy felt something cold like ice forming in the pit of her stomach. Then she rallied. "If nothing wrong is going on, then he does not have anything to worry about," she said stoutly.

"But perhaps you might find *you* have something to worry about." Belinda looked at her sister anxiously.

"I? Why?"

"Let us suppose it is a normal morning service. The Runners and the press burst in. Explanations are demanded. How did you come by this ridiculous story? The editor is approached. He will reveal that he sustained a visit from one Miss Lucy Bliss."

"But I have heard that the gentlemen of the press never reveal the source of their information."

"When faced with an angry duke, I cannot see any editor putting himself out to protect a green girl."

Lucy turned a trifle pale. Belinda squeezed her hand and said pratically, "Never mind. Let us just pray it *is* a black mass. Oh, here comes your Mr. Graham!"

Lucy gave him a warm welcome and asked him if there was somewhere they could be private. Gratified, Mr. Graham looked around him. He could not take Lucy off to a room somewhere in the house: that would cause a scandal. But over in the corner was a bank of hothouse palms. He led her behind them.

"I am much concerned about Wardshire," began Lucy.

Mr. Graham felt a stab of pure jealousy. Wardshire! Always Wardshire.

"What about him?" he asked huffily.

"Is he . . . is he really such a monster? Belinda says that such as he would find a black mass too undignified."

Mr. Graham was about to say that Miss Belinda had a great deal of good sense but then reflected that Wardshire had actually asked to have his reputation blackened, and besides, pretty Miss Bliss should not be thinking about him so much.

"Well, don't you know, I'm fond of him," he said, adopting a judicious air, "and I ain't around when he's getting up to the worst of his capers. I've heard about them, though. I cannot describe them to you, for they are not fit for gentle ears."

Lucy let out a slow breath of relief. This man was

Wardshire's closest friend. She had done the right thing.

And then, like some matriarchal jungle animal, Mrs. Bliss's fat face appeared between the palm leaves. "Why, Mr. Graham!" she cooed. "How naughty of you."

"Only talking, madam," Mr. Graham hurriedly said, and made his escape. He planned to ask Mrs. Bliss if he could take Lucy driving again, but wanted to do so when she was engaged with other company so that he would not have to listen to her going on and on.

On emerging from the palms, he bumped into Lady Fortescue. She was looking magnificent in a gown of gold tissue, damped to reveal the curves of her body. "Where is your friend Wardshire?" she asked.

"Gone to the country," said Mr. Graham.

Her face fell. "When does he plan to return?"

"Any day now. Means to do the Season."

She linked her arm in his and said, "Walk with me for a little. I would ask your advice."

"By all means," said Mr. Graham, although he wished he could escape.

"I wonder if you could explain Wardshire's odd behavior. He called on me. He is still in love with me, you know, and yet at the Harbys' ball, he affected to pay court to the daughters of that vulgar woman."

"She *is* vulgar," agreed Mr. Graham, "but there is no denying that her daughters are charming."

"But so unsuitable. Even Wardshire cannot be contemplating marriage with a girl half his age."

"No knowing," said Mr. Graham, tugging at his cravat.

She sighed. "I was so much in love with him."

"Then why did you marry Fortescue?"

"Alas, that was the fault of my parents."

"Really?" Like the duke, Mr. Graham recalled the Bellinghams as a small, faded, timid couple. Had there not been some gossip that Clarinda Bellingham had behaved disgracefully during her first Season and that her parents had heaved a mighty sigh of relief when she had announced her intention of marrying Fortescue?

"I have never forgotten him," she said. "He may think I did not wait for him, but I have been cruelly punished, for I have waited all these years."

"I do not now what to say." Mr. Graham looked wildly around. "He does not confide in me."

Her large blue eyes seemed to swallow him up. "But *you* could confide in him. Tell him, dear Mr. Graham, that I am ready to marry him."

"Um, of course . . . delighted. If that's what you want."

Her grip on his arm grew tighter. "And you will call on me and let me know what he says?"

"Yes, ma'am. Must go. Someone looking for me." Mr. Graham made his escape. He could not see Lucy anywhere, but her sister was talking to several gentlemen, and so he joined the group about her. How refreshing the Bliss girls were after Lady Fortescue, he thought as Belinda gave him a warm smile. Emboldened by that smile, he asked her to promenade with him and felt very proud when she accepted and left her little group of courtiers to move off with him.

"Where is Lucy?" she asked.

He twisted his neck this way and that. "Disappeared somewhere," he said.

"I am very fond of her, you know," confided Belinda.

"As we all are, Miss Belinda."

She peeped up at him. "Even Wardshire? After that terrible drawing? Did he tell you about it?"

He gave a reluctant laugh. "Yes, he says he is going to have it framed."

"Lucy is a very clever artist," said Belinda. "I should think Wardshire is a very clever man, too. Such a pity about his reputation. But it is said he will probably marry Lady Fortescue."

"Perhaps not," said Mr. Graham cautiously.

"You were telling Lucy that Wardshire plans to hold a black mass this Sunday."

"Was I? Well, I may have said something like that."

"An odd thing to say about your closest friend even if it were true."

Mr. Graham looked about. "I say, look at Anstruther's coat. Quite disgraceful."

"We were talking about the duke's black mass," said Belinda firmly. "Had you not considered it might be a rather *dangerous* thing to tell such a high-spirited lady as my sister? Did it not occur to you that she might go to the authorities?"

Mr. Graham stopped dead and gave her a stricken look. "She didn't!"

"I am not saying she did."

"Oh, but she wouldn't."

"Could it be that you were lying, Mr. Graham?"

Mr. Graham thought rapidly. If Lucy had gone to the authorities, then surely he himself would already have been questioned. He felt himself relax. "Oh, Wardshire did say something about it. Wicked man! Don't bother your pretty head. Talk about something else."

And so Belinda dutifully talked about her impressions of London, and Mr. Graham began to find her much more attractive than Lucy, until Lucy came to join them and he realized with a shock that he was falling in love with her.

He thought guiltily about that black mass, but then mentally shrugged. He would tell Wardshire on his return what he had said, and they would have a laugh about it.

Mr. James Benson, reporter on the *Morning Bugle*, stood uneasily outside the gates of Sarsey with two Bow Street Runners. "You know why they gave me this job?" he demanded. "It's because they think I'm expendable."

"We're just here to do our duty, sir," said one of the Runners impassively.

"Yes, it's all very well for you," said Mr. Benson. "But I'm not bursting into that chapel."

"Then how," demanded the other Runner, "do you expect us to find out what's going on?"

"Let me see if there's any way I can have a look in first," pleaded Mr. Benson. "Now, where's this 'ere chapel?"

"Next the house," said one Runner, "and we're in luck. All the servants go, which means the lodge keeper and his family as well, so we just walk in."

Mr. Benson, sweating lightly with nerves, walked with them up the long, long drive. Daffodils were blowing in the tussocky grass, and forsythia bushes blazed in all their golden glory. It was a perfect spring day. Black mass, indeed. But the editor had told him that the information came from a young society lady, a Miss Lucy Bliss, so surely there must be something in it. On the other hand, society ladies read a great deal of Gothic novels. His thoughts churned round and round.

When they came to the chapel, he heaved a sigh of relief. At some point in the seventeenth century, the chapel had obviously been visited by Cromwell's soldiers, for several statues of saints on the outside of the small building had been defaced, and most important of all, there was only plain glass in the windows, and better and better, a ladder lay in the grass beside the chapel.

"Here," he said, "I have an idea. Help me put this ladder up against one of the windows and I'll have a look-see. If all's normal, we can just go quietly away."

They propped the long ladder against the ivy-covered wall, and Mr. Benson climbed slowly up until he could see in at the window.

The church was full of tenants and servants of the duke's estate, a sober, ordinary group of worshipers. The duke himself was reading the lesson, standing behind the great brass eagle which supported the family Bible. The vicar, a cherubic young man of patent respectability, stood beside the altar, on which the cross was definitely the right way up.

And as Mr. Benson from his perch looked down, the duke looked up and saw him. He shouted something and pointed at the window. Mr. Benson let out a cry and tried to nip down the ladder, missed his footing, and fell with a crash to the ground as the chapel doors opened and the congregation came streaming out.

He felt sick and dizzy as he sat up and looked blearily at the ring of faces around him. And then, there, glaring down at him, was the satanic Duke of Wardshire. The duke jerked the unfortunate reporter to his feet and shook him hard. "Explain yourself," he roared.

"Here's two Runners, Your Grace," shouted a voice.

The duke dropped Mr. Benson, who sank down on the grass with a moan, and marched toward the Runners, who doffed their wide hats and bowed.

"It's like this, Your Grace," said one. "The editor of the *Morning Bugle* called at Bow Street and says how there's a report that you were to hold a black mass here. Had to investigate."

"I think you had better come indoors, and bring that churl of a reporter with you," snapped the duke.

Mr. Benson found himself sitting on a chair in one of the state rooms of Sarsey. The grandeur of the surroundings was intimidating and he gratefully seized the glass of brandy being held out to him by a footman and drank it in one gulp.

"Now, young man," said the duke. "Out with it. Who started this slander?"

"It was a Miss Lucy Bliss," Mr. Benson bleated, and cowered as the duke's face appeared to grow dark with rage. "She came into the editor's office and told him, and he went to Bow Street. Your Grace, I felt sure it was all lies and they were only sending me because I'm new and so it wouldn't hurt to get rid of me. So I suggested to the Runners that I should climb up to the window of the chapel and have a look, and if all was normal, we could leave quietly. But . . . but . . . you saw me and I got a fright and fell off the ladder."

The Runners, stolidly drinking ale, seemed indifferent both to their surroundings and the reporter's plight.

Mr. Benson looked pleadingly toward the footman who refilled his glass. The duke strode up and down. His temper was cooling. After all, had he not brought all this on himself? Had he not fostered such a black reputation, then Bow Street would simply have laughed at Miss Bliss's story.

But the Bliss family deserved to be punished, and punished they would be. They were at fault, not this young man.

He swung round and said in a mild voice to Mr. Benson, "I would like you to write something after all."

"Anything," gasped Mr. Benson, who had been fearing a horsewhipping.

"Then go over to the desk and take down what I dictate."

The duke waited until he was ready and then began to ruin the Bliss family. He explained he had built up a bad reputation for himself to protect himself from encroaching mushrooms like Mrs. Bliss. He had not expected that disgraceful family would perpetrate the ultimate vulgarity on him of sending the Runners to disturb his morning service.

By the time he had finished writing, Mr. Benson was praising God more fervently than anyone in the congregation had done earlier. What a story!

Three people were relieved when Sunday passed without incident–Mr. Graham, Lucy, and Belinda. Lucy came to the conclusion that the editor had damned her privately as a silly, hysterical female and had done nothing about it. She began to feel silly herself and could only be grateful that the sinister duke would never know of her folly. Meanwhile, Almack's opening ball, to be held on that Wednesday, was looming.

And then Black Monday dawned.

Lucy started from sleep as scream after scream rent the house.

Mrs. Bliss did not read the *Morning Bugle*, but her butler did. He carried the paper up to his mistress's bedchamber, opened it, and pointed solemnly to the duke's story.

That was when Mrs. Bliss started to scream.

Lucy ran to her mother's bedchamber. Feathers was already there, holding smoking brown paper under her mistress's nose, which made the screaming Mrs. Bliss subside into coughs and splutters. Belinda, pretty in a rose pink wrapper, was hovering anxiously by the bed. Mr. Bliss in his undress was urging his wife to calm herself.

With a shaking finger, Mrs. Bliss pointed to the newspaper on the bed. All gathered round and read it.

"Goodness, he really is wicked after all," exclaimed Belinda. "What a revenge. We are socially ruined." She sounded quite cheerful.

"There, now," said Mr. Bliss. "It is no great matter. We will retire to the country and wait until everyone forgets this scandal."

"All my work, all my hopes," moaned Mrs. Bliss. "Lucy, you are a wicked, wicked girl and I will *never* forgive you."

"But Mr. Graham told me he was holding a black mass," shouted Lucy, white with anger and despair. "He told me!"

"And you fool, you listened to him," declared Mrs. Bliss. "Get out of my sight."

It became a house of mourning that day. The shutters were closed and the blinds drawn down. And then a message arrived from Almack's to say that the vouchers for the Bliss family had been canceled "under the circumstances." Mrs. Bliss's humiliation was complete.

Lucy could have borne it if her mother had continued to shout and accuse. But Mrs. Bliss had fallen silent for the first time anyone could remember. She shut herself in her room for two days, seeing no one but Feathers.

On Wednesday afternoon she emerged and summoned her daughters. "There is only one thing to be done," she announced.

"Go back to the country?" suggested Belinda hopefully.

"Not like this. Not in disgrace. We must throw ourselves on Wardshire's mercy."

"He will just laugh at you, Mama," said Lucy.

Mrs. Bliss crossed to her desk with a firm, determined tread. "I shall not retreat without fighting. He will come, you'll see. I will ask him to present himself here and beg his forgiveness."

Belinda drew her protesting sister from the room. "Do not become exercised over it," she whispered. "He will not even deign to reply."

And the duke did not mean to. He read the letter as he was preparing to go to Almack's and then dropped it in the fire.

He would not admit to himself that he was still furious at Lucy Bliss.

And then Mr. Rufus Graham called to accompany him to Almack's.

"See you've been making a splash in the newspaper," said Mr. Graham awkwardly. "Deuced hard on the Bliss girls."

"The article was directed against Lucy Bliss in particular. That minx was out to try to ruin me, so she got ruined instead."

Mr. Graham looked miserable. "It's all my fault."

"How so?"

"Well, you know how you've always asked me to help blacken your reputation. Well, I took Miss Bliss, Lucy, out for a drive and she asked me if you were as black as you had been painted. So I told her you were holding a black mass on Sunday and threw in a possible human sacrifice for good measure."

"And the silly little fool *believed* you?"

"Why not?" demanded Mr. Graham defensively. "Ain't you gone on for years as if you were Lucifer himself? And have you not realized that Miss Bliss will do anything to protect her sister, Belinda, from the likes of you? Now, with most other ladies, your reputation wouldn't matter any more than it does to Mrs. Bliss, but these are *good* girls. I know Mrs. Bliss is vulgar, but she is simply more open about things than most other mothers at the Season. She is of no account. But you are a duke, and your revenge was more than even such as Mrs. Bliss deserved—a cannon to slaughter a gnat."

"What's done is done," said the duke quietly. "You may restore the Bliss fortunes this evening by dancing with Miss Lucy Bliss, but I, thank goodness, am finished with that family for good. Mrs. Bliss even had the temerity to *write* to me, asking me to call."

"Stands to reason. You've not only got your revenge on her and Miss Bliss but on poor Belinda and that quiet little Mr. Bliss."

"The matter is closed," said the duke harshly. "Let us see what Almack's has to offer."

Chapter Five

IT SHOULD HAVE crossed the duke's mind that his famous newspaper interview had given the patronesses of Almack's the opportunity they craved—that of spurning the Bliss family—but it did not. He tried to put the fragile and elfin figure of Lucy Bliss from his mind, but his eyes kept ranging around Almack's looking for her, and every time he looked, he only noticed that Lady Fortescue was trying to get his attention.

He began to feel himself becoming angry and would not admit that his growing anger was prompted by guilt. How could he ever have indulged in such folly as encouraging either Lady Fortescue or the ambitions of such as Mrs. Bliss?

He suddenly had no interest in Lady Fortescue whatsoever. He did not want revenge on her. He had been a green youth when he had proposed to her. It was not her fault that he had not at that time recognized the shallowness of her character. He had come to the Season with the express purpose of finding himself a bride, but all the debutantes looked the same: same plump arms, same white muslin dresses, same simpering expressions. Not one of them had the wide, direct gaze of Lucy Bliss.

Damn Lucy Bliss!

Yet he made his way to Mrs. Drummond Burrell's side, although still convincing himself that it was only polite to pay his courtesies to this formidable patroness, and found himself saying, "It is nearly eleven o'clock. The doors will soon be closed. If Mrs. Bliss plans to make one of her entrances, she had better be quick about it."

"My dear Wardshire!" Mrs. Drummond Burrell raised her eyebrows. "After what you revealed to the newspapers! The first thing I did was to withdraw her vouchers. And," she added with satisfaction, "I should hope the Bliss family will be clever enough to leave town very soon, for all are withdrawing their invitations."

"That is a trifle harsh," he murmured.

"Harsh? My dear duke, we all share your views. These pushing mushrooms and counter-jumpers must be kept in their place."

"But Bliss is of the untitled aristocracy, and Mrs. Bliss of the gentry," he pointed out.

"Then Bliss should control his wife, and his wife should behave in the manner of the gentry," she said severely. "But I must not keep you." She looked at him slyly. "Here comes one who is of more interest to you."

With a sinking heart, the duke saw Lady Fortescue bearing down on him.

"Wardshire!" she trilled. "We are all talking about that article in the newspaper. Such a delight to see the pretentious Mrs. Bliss trounced! And you, you wicked man, to lead society by the nose with fictitious tales of your evildoing."

They walked a little way away from the curious ears of Mrs. Drummond Burrell. "You have not asked me to dance," teased Lady Fortescue. "Nor any other lady."

He looked around the ballroom with a scowl.

"I' faith, my lady," he said, "I made a sad mistake in coming to town."

"How so?"

"I had convinced myself that my bachelor state displeased me. Now I find it infinitely desirable."

Two spots of color burned on her cheeks. "You are blunt," she said. "You led me to believe otherwise."

"A malicious trick for which I am truly sorry," he said. "You snubbed me once. I was taking my revenge."

Before she could stop herself, she had slapped his face.

And that slap rang around the ballroom. She had slapped him just at a point when Neil Gow's band had ceased to play. Faces turned, mouths dropped open, quizzing glasses were raised, and a hum of gossip and speculation rose to the huge crystal chandelier.

He turned on his heel and walked out. He felt he must be losing his wits. Whatever had possessed him to be so blunt?

Mr. Graham caught up with him. "Let's go to the club," he said. "It's all so damned flat without the Bliss girls, although I don't expect you to agree." Mr. Graham was very relieved he had not told the duke that Lady Fortescue expected to marry him.

The duke said nothing but strode on while Mr. Graham, impeded by all the fashionable discomforts of tight corset and false calves, struggled to keep up.

* * *

The next day Mrs. Bliss sat at her desk, gloomily looking at a small pile of invitation cards she had taken down from the mantelpiece. All invitations had been canceled. But to retreat to the country, beaten! To face the syrupy sympathy of her friends, who would all have read that newspaper article. Everyone professed loudly that they would not dream of reading such a low, common, radical paper as the *Morning Bugle*, but most did. Mrs. Bliss felt tears rising to her eyes and angrily brushed them away. Belinda should have been at Almack's. Belinda would have been the star of Almack's. And all, all ruined because of Lucy. Mr. Graham had called several times asking permission to take Lucy on a drive, but Mrs. Bliss had refused each time. Why should Lucy have a beau when she had ruined Belinda's chances of ever making a match? And it was of no use talking to Belinda. All Belinda would say in her placid way was that any man really interested in her would not pay any heed to either gossip or newspaper articles.

Mrs. Bliss thought and thought and then, ever optimistic, came to the conclusion that the Duke of Wardshire did not realize the full extent of the damage he had done. And had he not shown himself to be smitten by Belinda? Mrs. Bliss squared her plump shoulders. Like the Duke of Wellington, she would show that action was the best form of defense. She would go to the duke's town house and lay the matter before him.

The duke had never dreamt that Mrs. Bliss would have the temerity to call on him at his London home and so had given the servants no instructions to send her away. So when Mrs. Bliss made her call, saying it was most important, the butler did not really know what to do. He, of course, had read that newspaper article, and therefore it surely stood to reason that the duke would not relish seeing her. The duke was out, but Mrs. Bliss, accompanied by Feathers, said firmly that she would wait, and noticing the butler's worried look, added calmly, "His Grace is expecting my call."

The butler's face cleared. He put Mrs. Bliss and Feathers in the drawing room, furnished them with wine and cakes, and withdrew.

Mrs. Bliss sat and planned her strategy. She was now inside the house—the house that could have been Belinda's, as well as Sarsey. The drawing room was immense, with little islands of tables and chairs dotted here and there. Everything was of the finest, and the furniture was modern. But it had an impersonal air, and Mrs. Bliss suspected that the room was hardly ever used.

Deaf to the mutterings of Feathers, who was complaining that the duke would simply order his servants to throw Mrs. Bliss out, Mrs. Bliss did not bother to point out that she had already made plans to thwart such a happening. She sat in a chair by a long window that overlooked the street, a formidable matron in plum velvet with an awesome turban on her head ornamented with one tall peacock's feather, which bobbed and twitched with every movement as if trying to fly away and escape from imprisonment on top of this human body.

Mrs. Bliss looked down from her vantage point, and after half an hour was rewarded by the sight of the Duke of Wardshire driving up.

She opened her capacious reticule and, taking out a small flask of onion juice, liberally dabbed her eyes with it before throwing the rest of the contents into poor Feathers's startled face.

With tears streaming from her eyes, Feathers groped her way downstairs after her mistress, wondering whether Mrs. Bliss had run mad.

So just as the duke's butler was about to tell His Grace of the visitors, the duke found himself confronted by Mrs. Bliss, weeping copiously, followed by an equally lachrymose maid, and both smelling vilely of onions.

Mrs. Bliss sank to her fat knees and held up her chubby, velvet-covered arms. "I fall on your mercy, Your Grace!"

"Control yourself, madam," snapped the duke. "Nothing irritates me more than a crying female." That had the effect of making Mrs. Bliss quickly dry her eyes, although poor Feathers, who had suffered from the brunt of the onion juice, continued to weep. "And pray rise. I shall spare you ten minutes. No, do not go above again. The library will suffice." He opened a door that led off the hall. Mrs. Bliss marched in, her mind working furiously.

When she was seated, the duke stood in front of the fireplace and looked down at her. "Before you speak, if you have come to complain to me about your social downfall, then may I point out that it was up to you to bring up your daughters, or rather your elder daughter, to be better behaved?"

"I have done my best. But it was you, as you admitted to the newspaper, that started the tales of your villainy, Your Grace, and poor Lucy believed them, particularly as your own best friend told her that you were to hold a black mass. I fear Lucy has been more sinned against than sinning.

"Furthermore, if I am such a poisonous mushroom, why did you choose to call on me? If you had taken me and my family in dislike, then all you had to do was stay away."

The duke found himself becoming strangely embarrassed. This ridiculous matron was only speaking the truth. He felt the beginnings of an odd respect for her. She was as single-minded in her aims as any general going in to battle.

All he had to do was to ring the bell and ask the servants to show her out, and that would be that. But the malicious imp which had prompted him to call on her in the first place, which had also prompted him to take revenge on Lady Fortescue, started to work again.

He suddenly smiled at her and said, "There is a way in which your social fortunes might be mended, madam, a way which would suit us both. I came to London to find a bride and have already discovered the task wearisome. Therefore, to make amends to you and for you to make amends to me, the only solution is that you give me your daughter's hand in marriage."

Mrs. Bliss stared at him, amazed, one plump hand going to her well-upholstered bosom. The duke had the satisfaction of seeing her struck speechless.

"So," went on the duke blandly, "perhaps you will explain matters to Mr. Bliss and tell him that I will call on him this afternoon to talk about the marriage settlements."

Mrs. Bliss felt that all the angels were singing for her. Belinda would be a duchess. Real tears of gratitude entered her eyes. But she said with some dignity, "We shall expect you, Your Grace. A *most* satisfactory arrangement."

"Now, why on earth did I do that?" mused the

duke when she had left. "I shall not actually go through with it as far as the altar, but it will restore that horrible family in the eyes of society, and yes, I think, provide me with some much-needed amusement."

Shortly afterwards, the Bliss household was in an uproar. Only Belinda, sitting in the middle of the small group composed of distressed father, furious sister, defiant mother, and red-eyed maid, appeared calm.

"How dare you!" shouted Mr. Bliss, his calm and timid world shattered. "How dare you sacrifice Belinda to such a man? He's nearly twice her age. Give my permission? Damn, I'll send the fellow, duke or no duke, to the right-about."

"And so what becomes of my girls?" demanded Mrs. Bliss, bosom heaving. "Because of your ingratitude, they will be cast into outer darkness."

"Only back to the country," snapped Lucy. "Mama, how could you be so foolish? He is amusing himself at your expense."

"No one has asked me what I think," put in Belinda and all surveyed her in surprise.

"Well, what *do* you think?" prompted Lucy.

"Sarsey is a very big place," said Belinda in a thoughtful voice. "One could disappear in such a place for days and days and be alone and quiet. I think being a duchess would suit me very well."

"There you are!" screamed Mrs. Bliss in delight. "There you are, Mr. Bliss! She wants him."

Mr. Bliss looked sorrowfully at Belinda. "Are you very sure?"

"Yes, Papa, for I would have a home of my own and perhaps one or two babies, although I would like a little dog first. You know Mama would never let me have one. But I could have lots of dogs at Sarsey, for I would be a duchess."

"But, my child, there is more to marriage than pets and babies. You make it sound like playing with a doll's house," said Mr. Bliss, and Lucy realized with a start of surprise that what he said was true. Belinda switched from grave maturity one moment to childishness the next, hovering, it seemed, between schoolroom and ballroom.

"I don't know what all the fuss is about," said Belinda. "He wants to marry me. I want to get away . . . I mean, it would be pleasant to have a home of my own, and perhaps Lucy to stay with me for very long visits. Yes, I should like that."

The rage that had seemed to animate Mr. Bliss and give him color faded away, and he sank back into his former gray, timid state.

"Very well," he said sadly, "I shall see Wardshire when he calls."

Lucy would have liked to talk to Belinda, but Belinda was swept off by Mrs. Bliss to prepare for the duke's proposal. Lucy felt very low in spirits.

Other girls of her class rarely saw their mothers from the cradle to the grave. Why was she cursed with such an overwhelming, talkative, brash, and vulgar mama? If Mrs. Bliss had not gone to see Wardshire, if Wardshire had not decided to continue his revenge against the Bliss family—for Lucy was sure it was part of a plan of revenge—then they would have gone back to their quiet life in the country.

She was leaving the drawing room when she heard someone arriving in the hall below. Thinking the duke had arrived early, she looked over the banisters and saw Mr. Graham and heard the butler saying regretfully, "I am afraid the ladies are not at home."

Lucy ran lightly down the stairs. "Oh, yes, we are," she said.

Mr. Graham brightened at the sight of her. "I have been calling and calling," he said. "I kept hoping to find you at home."

"And now you have," said Lucy. "Come to the drawing room. I need to talk to you." And under the butler's disapproving eye, she led him up the stairs.

"You will never guess what has happened," cried Lucy, "or do you already know what Wardshire has done?"

"Oh, that awful newspaper article," said Mr. Graham. "I must apologize, Miss Bliss. I did not intend to lie to you, but Wardshire had always told me to maintain the fiction of his villainy."

"Not that. Mama went to see him this morning to try to repair our social fortunes, and Wardshire says he will do it by marrying Belinda."

Mr. Graham looked at her in amazement. "Is he serious about it?"

"I suppose so, and yet I feel he plans to humiliate us further."

"And what of poor Miss Belinda? What does she say?"

"That's the trouble. She says she will accept him. But you see, Belinda craves a home of her own, and she is still part child in that she thinks only of having peace and quiet and being allowed to keep a dog. He will terrify her!"

"I do not think so," said Mr. Graham cautiously.

"He is actually very kind and generous, but perhaps prone to mischief, I admit."

"A mischief which will ruin my sister's happiness."

Mrs. Bliss came hurtling into the room. She moved always with a fast but fluid movement, rather like an overstuffed armchair on casters.

"Lucy, you should not entertain gentlemen callers unchaperoned, and you should know better, Mr. Graham. I must send you on your way. This is a great day for us, and there is much to do. Lucy, go abovestairs immediately. You cannot receive His Grace in that old gown."

And so Mr. Graham was shooed out.

Lucy submitted to being primped and preened with very bad grace—"particularly as you smell most vilely of onions, Feathers."

And so Feathers, heating the curling tongs on a small spirit stove, told Lucy how she came to be smelling of onions, and Lucy shuddered at this further proof of her mother's vulgarity. She prayed the duke had already had his revenge and that he would not call.

But at two o'clock Feathers whispered to her that the duke had arrived and was talking to Mr. Bliss, and Mrs. Bliss had said that Lucy must present herself in the drawing room.

In the drawing room Belinda was calmly stitching at a piece of tapestry while Mrs. Bliss paced up and down. The duke and Mr. Bliss were in the study downstairs. The minutes ticked by until a whole hour had passed, and Mrs. Bliss was beside herself with anxiety and worry, saying over and over again, "If your father has talked him out of it, I will never forgive him."

And then she stopped and listened. Footsteps were mounting the stairs. Mr. Bliss entered, followed by the duke.

"I am afraid there has been some mistake, my dear," said Mr. Bliss.

Mrs. Bliss let out a faint scream and sank down into an armchair. Lucy glared at the duke, who smiled back.

"It is not Belinda the duke wishes to marry," said Mr. Bliss. "He wishes to marry Lucy."

"Lucy!" shouted Mrs. Bliss.

"I?" said Lucy faintly.

Belinda went on stitching. She seemed mildly amused.

Lucy glared at the duke. "But I do not want to marry you," she cried.

He sighed. "What a pity. Then it will have to be Belinda."

"Oh, no." Lucy looked at her father. "Anything but that."

Her father came to her and took both her hands in his. "Listen, my dear, Wardshire is all that is considerate. He does not wish to rush you into things. You and he need to get to know each other better. To that end, he has invited us all to Sarsey so that you can be instructed in the running of a great house and . . . and to see how you go on."

Lucy twisted her hands in his. If she said no, then the duke would marry Belinda, and Belinda would accept and Belinda would be ruined. So she must pretend to accept his proposal and then give him such a disgust of her that he would cheerfully terminate the engagement.

Mrs. Bliss was making small moaning sounds from behind the barrier of a handkerchief.

"Yes," said Lucy, her quiet voice dropping like stone. "Yes, on reflection, I will marry you, Your Grace."

He smiled blandly on all. "May I then have a word in private with my fiancée?"

Mrs. Bliss was suddenly transformed from broken matron to triumphant matron. "Of course," she said smoothly. "Come, Belinda."

Lucy and the duke were left alone.

"What is your ploy?" asked Lucy wearily.

He looked down at her with a hint of compassion in his eyes. "Why, I think we should suit very well."

"I am sure you will find we will not," said Lucy. "You do not care a fig for me, sir. In fact, I am persuaded you are still looking for revenge."

"I? Fiddlesticks!"

"Then, my lord innocence, *why*?"

"Because I want to get married. You interest me, and I am persuaded you will not bore me."

Their eyes met in a long stare, and battle was declared.

Lucy suddenly smiled at him. "Then, sir, may I remind you, you have not proposed to me?"

His eyes glinted with amusement. He got down on one knee in front of her and took her hand in his. "Miss Lucinda Bliss," he said solemnly, "will you do me the very great honor of bestowing on me your hand in marriage?"

"Yes," said Lucy coldly.

He rose to his feet and drew her into his arms and bent his mouth to kiss her, but she jerked her face away and the kiss landed somewhere near her ear. He laughed and took her chin in his hand and held her firm. Then he kissed her mouth, warmly and sweetly, finally drawing back to leave her breathless and trembling.

"I see I do not leave your senses unaffected," he said. Lucy wiped her mouth with the back of her hand and glared at him. Her knees were shaking. How on earth was she going to win the battle if he was going to kiss her like that?

"I hope Miss Belinda is not too disappointed," he went on.

"Yes, I think she might be, a little," said Lucy. "She wanted a dog, you see, and marrying you was the only way she could think of getting one."

He threw back his head and laughed just as Mrs. Bliss, coughing in what she considered a discreet manner, entered the room, with Mr. Bliss and Belinda behind her.

Champagne was served and a toast drunk to the happy couple. It was agreed between the duke and Mrs. Bliss that all should travel to Sarsey on the following day.

"Tell me, Wardshire," said Lucy, "you plan to introduce me to the running of a very large house. I suggest you give me a free hand."

"Of course," he said smoothly, and then wondered what Miss Lucy Bliss was plotting.

Later that day he had to endure the wrath of Mr. Graham. Mr. Graham told him in no uncertain terms that he had upset Miss Bliss by proposing to Belinda. The duke reassured him by saying it was Lucy he was affianced to and then stared in amazement as Mr. Graham's normally calm and sheepish face grew scarlet in outrage.

"Your monster!" shouted Mr. Graham, marching off and leaving the duke to stare after him in bewilderment. Mr. Graham should have stayed to explain himself, to say that he himself was in love with Lucy. The duke would, in that case, have promptly canceled the engagement. He thought about his friend's anger and then decided that it was justified. He had been made to look a fool by that newspaper article, for was it not he who had told Lucy of the black mass?

The duke shrugged. He would see Rufus Graham when he returned from Sarsey and put matters to rights. Meanwhile, he was sure that Lucy had as little intention of marrying him as he had of her. He looked forward with great pleasure and anticipation to seeing how she would go about breaking the engagement.

He would not have felt quite so happy had he known where Rufus Graham had gone. Hurting and smarting, Mr. Graham found himself walking toward Manchester Square. For all at once he knew someone who would sympathize with his hurt.

Lady Fortescue was pleased to entertain him. She had been feeling very low after the scene at Almack's. She had been sternly reprimanded by one of the patronesses. She had a little hope that Mr. Graham was some sort of emissary from a repentant duke, but hope died when he blurted out that Wardshire was to wed Lucy Bliss.

"Not the pretty one!" exclaimed Lady Fortescue. "You mean the wispy one?"

"Be careful how you describe Miss Lucy Bliss to me," declared Mr. Graham. "For my heart is broken. He has stolen her from me."

Lady Fortescue felt a strong feeling of pique. Who was plain little Lucy Bliss to enchant men in this way? She began to wonder whether her own looking glass was lying to her and that she had grown old and ugly overnight.

She turned the battery of her charm on Mr. Graham, for there was only one true mirror, and that was to see herself reflected in a man's admiring eyes. "How betrayed you have been," she said. "How wicked of Wardshire." She took one of Mr. Graham's hands in hers. "And how wretched you must feel. Tell me all about it."

And so Mr. Graham did while those hypnotic blue eyes looked tenderly into his own. After talking for almost an hour, he found he could not quite recall what Lucy looked like. He seemed to be drowning bit by bit in those blue, blue eyes.

"Well, Mr. Graham will be sorely disappointed," said Lucy to Belinda. The hour was two in the morning, and they were both sitting on Lucy's bed.

"He was a little in love with you, I think." Belinda wrinkled her brow, fat little wrinkles on her soft skin like on the skin of the puppy she so longed to have.

"A little! I am persuaded, dear sister, that he was about to propose marriage."

"Perhaps it's best this way." Belinda gave a little sigh. "He was not for you."

"And I suppose Wardshire is?"

"Well, you know, Lucy, you are very high-spirited and clever, and so is he."

"That will not answer. Men detest clever women. Do you remember the Cartwright girls and their excellent governess? She taught them so well that Mrs. Cartwright became alarmed and gave the poor governess her marching orders, saying she had made the girls as intelligent as *men* and therefore unmarriageable. I plan to give Wardshire a disgust of me."

Belinda smiled at her sister placidly. "Do it quickly so that we can all be comfortable again."

Chapter Six

THE BLISS FAMILY and their host stopped for the night at a posting house on the road to Sarsey. Lucy was not obliged to make conversation over the dinner table, but then, with Mrs. Bliss around, very few people could manage to get the opportunity to say anything.

As usual, Lucy let the tide of her mother's voice wash over her, but suddenly sat up straight and listened when Mrs. Bliss said to the duke, "Of course, you may have no fear that Lucy will not be able to manage a large household. I shall be there to train her."

"No," said Lucy abruptly.

Mrs. Bliss stopped short. "I mean," said Lucy, "the housekeeper will be able to explain things to me. It would be better if I started on my own right away. I shall choose the menus, for example."

"A good idea," said the duke smoothly, although he wondered what Lucy was up to.

Lucy smiled and stood up. "Now, if you will excuse me . . ."

"Where are you going, Lucy?" demanded her mother.

"Really, Mama!" Lucy made for the door.

"Oh!" Mrs. Bliss colored, assuming that her daughter was going to the privy.

On their arrival at the posting house, Lucy had spied a likely couple in the common dining room. The duke's party was dining abovestairs in his private parlor. To her relief, the couple was still there, and as awful as she had remembered them to be.

The woman was tall and overdressed, with a common accent which strove ludicrously to be genteel. She had brassy blond hair under a huge bonnet ornamented with feathers died pink and purple, which clashed with her scarlet- and white-striped gown. Her eyelashes were so clogged with lampblack that they looked like spiders. Her bosoms, mostly bared by the lowness of her gown, were, Lucy judged, false ones, made of wax and strapped on. Her companion was a small, foxy man with sparse red hair, a crooked nose, and a knowing look.

Lucy approached them. "I beg your pardon," she said. "I saw you earlier and was taken by the cut of your gown, madam. I am Miss Lucy Bliss. I wonder whether you would be so good as to furnish me with the name of your dressmaker."

"Charmed," said the lady. "But I would not betray the name of my dressmaker, not if you brought in wild 'orses to drag it out o' me. I'm Mrs. Hardacre, and this is my . . . husband, Mr. Jonas Hardacre."

Mr. Hardacre shot to his feet and bowed so low that his nose touched the table.

"Do you belong to these parts?" asked Lucy.

"Naw. We're stoppin' here for a few days afore going on south," said Mr. Hardacre. "What's it to you?"

"I shall be honest with you. I am affianced to the

Duke of Wardshire, whose home, Sarsey, is four hours ride from here. I shall have the running of his house and would like to see how I can manage a little dinner party. You seem to me so congenial, so lively—for I am of a timid disposition, you know—I wondered whether you would honor me with a visit."

"To Sarsey?" Mr. Hardacre's little eyes were hard and bright.

"Yes, tomorrow evening. We shall keep city hours, I think. Dinner at seven."

Mrs. Hardacre visibly preened. "Well, I don't know, I'm sure, but seeing at how you put it like that, I'm sure we would be delighted to obleege."

"We'll be there," said Mr. Hardacre.

Lucy curtsied to both of them and then darted back up the stairs, where she re-joined the others and sat down at the table with such an air of meek docility that the duke looked at her suspiciously.

Later, in the room that she shared with Belinda, Lucy told her sister what she had done. "And they are so deliciously vulgar," crowed Lucy. "He will be furious with me. And just wait until you see the menu I have planned for dinner!"

Belinda looked at her sister doubtfully. "Do not go too far, Lucy. I should hate to see Wardshire in a temper. I do not think that would be very pleasant at all!"

They arrived at Sarsey the following morning. After a cold collation, the duke suggested that they all might like to retire to their rooms, for they had left the posting house early. But Lucy said meekly that she would like to start her training right away by choosing the menu for dinner.

Lucy sat in the study downstairs while the chef and the housekeeper were ushered in. Both stood before her with impassive faces while Lucy wrote down the menu. "I think we should begin with calf's-head soup," she said, "and then perhaps broiled mackerel after that. For the main dish, broiled bacon cheek, and then as a dessert, bread-and-butter pudding."

Housekeeper and chef stared at her stolidly. "You see," said Lucy, smiling on them, "I do not believe in extravagant meals."

"Very good, miss," said the housekeeper. "How many will there be at dinner?"

"Myself and my family and His Grace and two guests. Perhaps you should ask His Grace whether he wishes to invite anyone. Any questions?"

"No, miss," said the housekeeper. "Will that be all?"

"Perhaps you would like to take me on a tour of the house and show me where everything is," said Lucy.

The housekeeper, a Mrs. Budge, beamed her approval. "We can start right away, miss."

And unaware that she was making a favorable impression on the servants, Lucy began her tour of the great house. The chef was impressed by her choice of simple fare, which he regarded as a challenge to his art. Also, if this future duchess was going to specialize in ordering only the simplest of items, it meant that the chef, Monsieur Pierre, could put some money in his own pockets. All the servants to whom Lucy was introduced by Mrs. Budge thought she was already like a duchess and had a commanding ease of manner. Had Lucy really been on trial, she would have been terrified, but as it was, it was all just a game to her. As she moved from great room to great room, she reflected that it was just as well she was not going to be a duchess, for the house was vast, with its picture galleries, long galleries, and chains of saloons and drawing rooms, and quite intimidating.

The duke was later informed that Miss Bliss had invited two guests for dinner. He wondered who on earth they could be and then reflected that as Sarsey was in driving distance from Lucy's country home, she had no doubt invited two of her friends.

Lucy had meanwhile descended to the kitchens and exclaimed over the open fire—albeit one with a clockwork spit—that Monsieur Pierre must have one of the new closed stoves. Open fires were dangerous, and what were called hearth deaths were all too common, servants' clothes often going ablaze. The Bodley Range was the best model. Monsieur Pierre demurred, saying that the Bodley Range used a prodigious twelve to fifteen scuttles of coal a day, whereupon Lucy said blithely that the duke could well afford the expense, therefore negating her earlier claims of thrift.

As his fiancée was obviously taken up with household matters, the duke escorted the rest of the Bliss family around the gardens. Mrs. Bliss exclaimed loudly at everything. Lucy was obviously, for the first time ever, the favorite daughter, and Mrs. Bliss, when not casting a proprietorial eye over plants and bushes, sang her praises. The duke, then wearying of Mrs. Bliss, suggested, as Lucy was occupied, that he take Belinda on a visit to the vicar. He somehow made it quite plain that he did not include Mr. and Mrs. Bliss in the invitation.

Mrs. Bliss talked feverishly while they waited for

the duke's carriage to be brought round. She fussed over Belinda, sending her upstairs to find a warm shawl to put about her, although the day was fine and warm. When the duke finally drove off, Belinda gave a happy little sigh as her mother's voice faded in the distance.

"What is the vicar's name?" she asked.

"Mr. Peter Marsham, a young fellow, not married and therefore pursued ruthlessly by the maids of the parish."

"How wretched this marriage business is," said Belinda.

"Indeed! What an odd thing to say when your own sister is about to wed me."

"It is not as if you or Lucy is in love," said Belinda.

He experienced a momentary flash of anger. "Then why is she marrying me?"

"To prevent your marrying *me*," she said equably. "You did say you would take me if she didn't want you."

"Do you mean Lucinda does *not* want to marry me?"

"At the moment, no," said Belinda. "But you could change that, I think, if you wished, but you don't wish. You have saved the social name of Bliss, and it will still be saved when you get Lucy to cry off, and then we can all be comfortable again."

Having his intentions so plainly read by a mere child of a girl was very lowering for the duke. "Tell me," he said, "what type of man would Miss Lucy like to marry?"

"Someone like you, I think," said Belinda earnestly. "Such a pity you went about things the wrong way. Oh, do look at that deer. So graceful!"

He burst out laughing, amused by her mixture of wisdom and naïveté. But he then thought that if Belinda had so correctly guessed his intentions, then Lucy must have guessed them as well.

"Does your sister know that I do not mean to marry her?" he asked.

"No. Lucy is hoping to give you a disgust of her. But please do not tell her you don't want to marry her."

"Why, pray?"

"Because you might fall in love with her, and then you might wish you had never said anything."

"Are you usually so forthright?"

She wrinkled her brow and sighed. "Not always. Mrs. Cartwright, now, she asked me last month what I thought of her bonnet, which was quite dreadful, being of a dismal shade of puce with brown flowers, and I said it was delightful. But these circumstances are so odd. You and Lucy are very alike with your games and strategems. Perhaps you should really marry each other. Either of you would give anyone else a hard time of it. Is this the vicarage?"

The carriage had stopped in front of a stone house so covered in ivy that it was hard to guess the age of the building.

The duke held open the garden gate for Belinda. He knocked on a low door and it was answered by a grim maid of indeterminate years and surpassing ugliness. Belinda wondered whether the vicar had hired the one woman in the local parish who would not nourish hopes of marriage, for it was well known that any single churchman became the romantic object of servant and mistress alike.

They were ushered into a low-ceilinged, stone-flagged parlor which had a dismal, well-scrubbed air. The servant left them, and after a few moments the door opened and a young man entered. Mr. Peter Marsham had a head of golden curls, wide blue eyes, and a cherubic, innocent appearance. He bowed low before the duke and Belinda and then sat down nervously on the very edge of a chair.

He appeared very overawed by the duke, thought Belinda as, after the introductions, the vicar answered plain yes and no to various questions. The duke, however, blamed the beautiful Belinda for the vicar's unease. Usually he and Mr. Marsham talked like old friends. He almost wished he had brought Mrs. Bliss with him.

And then from somewhere at the back of the house came the sounds of shrill barking.

"Oh, have you dogs!" breathed Belinda, clasping her hands, her eyes shining.

"I have a collie bitch," said the vicar. "She has recently whelped, but I do not know who the father is. The pups look most odd. I suppose I must find homes for them."

"Could I see them?" pleaded Belinda.

"Of course, Miss Belinda. But they are in the kitchen in a basket. Perhaps Mrs. George could—"

But Belinda was already on her feet. "Oh, I must see them, Mr. Marsham. Pray lead the way."

Mr. Marsham jumped to his feet as well and knocked over a small table in his agitation. Then he stumbled into the door and, blushing and breathless, managed to open it and usher his guests through.

The kitchen was much larger than the parlor, and at the back of the house. It contained a quantity of black iron implements from the last century, larding needles, skillets, brandreths, griddles, and pot hangers. The table was scrubbed, and the chairs, hard and upright. The floor had been sanded.

In the corner lay the collie beside a large wicker basket out of which four sleepy, yapping puppies were tumbling. The collie was gold and white. The puppies were an odd hairy mixture of black and white and gold, all with paws that seemed too big for them. One of the smallest lollopped toward Belinda, who bent down and scooped up the little creature with a cry of delight. "What is this one called?"

"That's Barney, the runt of the litter. Farmer Jones was saying I should drown 'em and get it over with, but I am persuaded some kind people may want to adopt my charges."

Belinda clutched the puppy in her arms. It wriggled ecstatically and licked her nose, and she gave a little crow of delight.

"Are they weaned?" asked the duke.

"Yes," said the vicar. "They're old enough for that."

"If only I could have this one," said Belinda.

"Pray do take it," said the vicar. "It would be one less for me to worry about."

Belinda looked pleadingly over the puppy's head at the duke. "Mama would never let me."

"Then I will present it to you to celebrate my forthcoming marriage."

The light went out of the vicar's eyes. "Am I to take it that congratulations are in order, Your Grace?"

"They are indeed, but not to Miss Belinda here, but to her elder sister."

"Then we must drink a toast," cried the vicar. "Mrs. George! The best cowslip wine."

They made their way back to the parlor, Belinda still clutching the puppy. The vicar managed to tread on the train of her white morning gown and stammered his apologies while Belinda smiled at him in a kindly way and said it did not matter at all.

Either it was the cowslip wine or the vicar was elated by Belinda's friendliness, but he started to talk at a great rate about the beauties of the parish, about the changing seasons, about how the country was infinitely more preferable to the town, and then asked Belinda shyly if she thought the vicarage too dark and poky, used as she obviously was to great houses.

"I think it is delightful," said Belinda, looking about her. "Or rather it could be. If I were here, I would put some pretty chintz covers on these chairs and make new curtains for the window." She put her head on one side consideringly. "Just a few touches, you know, a few bowls of flowers and some little ornaments."

The vicar clasped his hands and looked at her as she sat with the puppy in her lap. He had a vision of paradise, a paradise where he would sit in front of a cozy fire in the evenings working on his sermons while this pretty goddess sat opposite, sewing curtains.

"But you have not met Mama yet, you see," said Belinda, and the duke looked at her in surprise. It was as if Belinda had been replying to some question put to her by the vicar, and yet he had said nothing.

"Ah," said the vicar. "With such beauty, she must have very high hopes for you, Miss Belinda."

"She had," said Belinda, "but now that Lucy is

to marry a duke, I do not think she will be ambitious about me anymore. That is, so long as His Grace and Lucy do get married." She patted the puppy and said half to herself, "If Lucy were not to marry the duke, then Mama *would* become ambitious again, and what is more, she would make me get rid of this darling puppy. Yes, I see it all now. I am afraid, Your Grace, that you will have to marry Lucy after all."

"But is there some . . . doubt?" The vicar looked in a bewildered way from Belinda to the duke.

"Miss Belinda," said the duke severely, "do not addle my poor vicar's wits any more than you have already addled them. Marsham, we must take our leave. I called to invite you to dinner tonight. When do we dine, Miss Belinda?"

"I think Lucy said something about seven o'clock," said Belinda. She stood up, holding the puppy with one hand to her breast and holding out the other to the vicar. "Good-bye, Mr. Marsham. I am glad you are coming to dinner, for we are very much alike, and therefore I shall have someone to talk to. Not that it is very easy to talk when Mama is present, and goodness knows what sort of people Lucy is going to inflict on us."

"What sort of people?" asked the duke sharply.

Belinda smiled vaguely. "Come, Barney, and I will take you with me and find a basket for you. Will you miss your mother, I wonder? Not being married is so frustrating when it comes to keeping dogs, Mr. Marsham. Had I a complacent husband, then I could relieve you of the whole litter." She gave him a dazzling smile and he reddened and blinked as though in strong sunlight.

"Was I mistaken or did you just propose marriage to my poor impressionable vicar?" asked the duke as they drove away from the vicarage.

"I do not remember saying any such thing," said Belinda placidly. "What a dear doggie."

Mrs. Bliss could not object to Barney, for the duke declared it was his present to Belinda to celebrate his forthcoming marriage. She privately decided to get rid of the dog as soon as the wedding ceremony was safely over.

Lucy was amused and looked forward to meeting this vicar, particularly after Belinda whispered to her that she wished to be placed next to Mr. Marsham at dinner.

Usually Belinda waited for Feathers to choose a gown for her, but Lucy found her going through every dress in her wardrobe during the dressing hour and holding one gown after the other up against her and studying the effect in the glass.

"You are trying to impress him," accused Lucy. "What will Mama say? A mere vicar."

"I think the blue gauze," said Belinda, studying her reflection critically. "And Mama is so in alt over your success, Lucy, that she will not trouble about me."

"But what will happen when the engagement is off?"

"I will cross the bridge when I come to it," said Belinda placidly. "Oh, do look at Barney. Such intelligent eyes."

"And such an interesting way of chewing up the coverlet," Lucy observed. "As temporary chatelaine, I should inform you that you are about to let that dog ruin anything it wants. It should be in the stables."

"Barney can't go to the stables. He will soon miss

his mother. He had better stay close to me. You must not wear that gown, Lucy. It is gray and makes you look like a wraith. Here is that sage green silk which I never liked. Get Feathers to put a few tucks in it and wear it with your coral beads. Most fetching."

Lucy, who trusted her sister's dress sense more than her own, took the gown and summoned Feathers to make a few quick alterations.

When they were all at last gathered in the drawing room, Belinda with Barney on a silk ribbon leash, the butler entered and said to the duke, "Two persons have arrived, Your Grace. They say they have been invited for dinner."

"A Mr. and Mrs. Hardacre?" asked Lucy quickly.

"The same."

"Do show them up. I invited them."

Mr. and Mrs. Hardacre were ushered in. Lucy half closed her eyes. Mrs. Hardacre had exceeded her wildest hopes. She was wearing a purple gown embellished with emerald green bows. On her head was perched an enormous muslin cap decorated with bows of the same color as if she had been just attacked by some monstrous species of green fly. Mr. Hardacre was wearing black evening dress. The coat looked as if it had been tailored for a much larger man. He was rouged and painted, and his hair had been powered inexpertly so that his own red color shone through the flour. He had a large paste diamond in his cravat and large paste diamond rings on his fingers. He obviously thought he looked very fine.

"Lucy," moaned Mrs. Bliss faintly. "How *could* you!"

The vicar was ushered in behind them and was promptly approached by Belinda.

"How very kind of you to come, Mr. Hardacre," said Lucy. "May I present His Grace, the Duke of Wardshire. My mother and father, Mr. and Mrs. Bliss, and yonder is my sister, Belinda, and Mr. Marsham."

"You must find it ever so odd of us to pop in like this, Your Grace," said Mrs. Hardacre, "but when Miss Bliss told us how frit she was of this gurt mansion, we felt we just had to come along to support her."

"I gather your acquaintance with Miss Bliss is of short duration?"

Mrs. Hardacre said something like "Hunh?"

"Have you known Miss Bliss long?"

"Naw, the dear cheild approached me and Jimmy last night and said she was that took with us, she wanted to invite us. So here we are!"

"Yes, here you are," echoed the duke bleakly.

The butler announced dinner was served and they all filed in, the duke leading the way with Mrs. Bliss on his arm, Mr. Bliss escorting Lucy, Belinda with the vicar, and the Hardacres following up at the rear.

That the Hardacres were sorely disappointed with the fare served to them in a ducal mansion became evident from their remarks as modest course followed course. Mrs. Hardacre said sotto voce to Mr. Hardacre that it was obvious that even dukes fell on hard times, and Mr. Hardacre remarked he would have been better off selling some of his plate and putting a decent meal on the table.

For once Mrs. Bliss, that great vulgar embarrasser of society, were herself driven into silence by the conversation and behavior of Mrs. Hardacre. Each had a napkin, but the Hardacres spurned theirs and wiped their mouths on the tablecloth. Mrs. Hardacre drank a great deal and began to flirt with Mr. Bliss, who, to Lucy's surprise, parried her sallies expertly and even looked mildly amused.

The duke treated them courteously and suggested that instead of lingering over the port, the gentlemen should join the ladies in the drawing room after dinner.

Elated with wine and high society, Mrs. Hardacre offered to entertain them. She sang several ballads which were very naughty indeed, finishing one by putting a foot up on the chair next to Mr. Bliss, raising her skirts, and snapping her garter. The duke thought that Mrs. Hardacre—if Mrs. she was—was probably a professional performer. He envied his vicar, who sat beside Belinda and seemed enclosed in shining walls of happiness.

Lucy sat elegantly at her ease, applauding even the worst of Mrs. Hardacre's offerings. The duke thought she looked strangely pretty in the simple green gown and with her wide eyes shining with mischief. He decided to punish her for inviting the Hardacres.

At last he said to the Hardacres that he must retire and they reluctantly took their leave, obviously hoping for another invitation. But Lucy, under her calm exterior, had become horrified at what she had done and merely curtsied to both.

"I will escort you to your carriage myself," said the duke, and Mrs. Hardacre preened.

Their carriage turned out to be a very broken down rented affair. "Before you leave," said the duke to Mr. Hardacre, "I am afraid I must ask you to turn out your pockets."

"Your Grace!" exclaimed Mr. Hardacre. 'What can you mean?"

"You know. Items as follows—two silver snuffboxes, one Dresden figurine, and some of the silverware from the dinner table."

Mr. Hardacre opened his mouth to protest. "Come, my good fellow," urged the duke, "you would not want me to summon my servants to turn you upside down and shake you."

"Oh, go on, Jimmy," said Mrs. Hardacre. "The gig's up. Hand 'em over."

Mr. Hardacre emptied out his pockets and passed the items over. "You're a downy one," he said to the duke in reluctant admiration.

"Now you may go on your way," said the duke. "I need not tell you that if you show your face near my home again, I shall set the constable on you."

"Oh, we're off!" Mrs. Hardacre tossed her head and set her ridiculous bows bobbing wildly. "But I'm right sorry for that little lady who's marrying you."

The duke waited until their carriage had driven away and then went thoughtfully indoors. He had missed a scene. Mrs. Bliss was red-eyed and weeping, Lucy defiant, Mr. Bliss subdued, and Belinda and the vicar were talking away as if nothing else mattered but what each other said.

"I crave a word in private with my fiancée," said the duke.

"Oh, Your Grace," waited Mrs. Bliss, "she is such a green girl. Forgive her!"

The duke pointedly held open the door, and Lucy walked past him with her head high. He led the way into a vast, empty saloon. Now he will tell me to break the engagement, thought Lucy. It will be painful, like a visit to the dentist, but so wonderful when it is all over.

He shut the door and approached her. He swept her into his arms and, despite her stifled mumbles of protest, kissed her soundly. "My little darling," he said huskily when he raised his head at last. "You enchant me. Such concern for my welfare, ordering all those cheap dishes! And such democracy. The Hardacres were a splendid idea. I can never remember when I was last so amused."

Lucy struggled away from him. "What are you doing? What are you *saying*?"

He smiled down at her. "I have the happiness to tell you that I am in love with you and cannot wait to be married. I will obtain a special license from the bishop tomorrow. Oh, my heart. I know this news will make you as happy as it does me." He gathered her in his arms again.

"But . . ." squeaked Lucy.

He crushed her head against his chest, ignoring her struggles. "You will soon be mine. Soon you will lie naked in my arms. You will like that, will you not, my darling? Oh, Lucinda." And he jerked up her chin and smothered her alarmed protests with a deep and lingering kiss which left her so shaken that when he released her, she could only stare at him dumbly.

"Come," he said, urging her tottering steps forward. "We must tell your parents the news!"

Chapter Seven

THE ANNOUNCEMENT of a wedding to be held in a bare three weeks time threw Mrs. Bliss into an ecstatic flurry of planning. As Lucy stood beside the duke, occasionally giving fierce little tugs at her hand to try to release it from his, Mrs. Bliss's happy voice beat upon her ears.

"Of course, I was took aback, Your Grace, for first of all, I had St. George's, Hanover Square, in mind. I know that no one who is anyone gets married in church these days, but there is something grand about a church, you know, bells and incense and stained glass." She went on as if churches had been built only to please the fastidious eye of society. "But as you say your family chapel will be perfect. Perhaps a rustic theme? With garlands of wildflowers held by village maidens? Perhaps even a cow or two in the churchyard and bridesmaids à la bergère."

"I do not really think I would like to dress up as a shepherdess for Lucy's wedding," said Belinda consideringly. "And think of the feelings of the people of Mr. Marsham's parish. They will think you are making a game of them."

"Pooh!" Mrs. Bliss waved one plump hand in dismissal. "Who cares what a lot of peasants think?

They will do as they're told. But the dress! Monsieur Farré must post down from London with his seamstresses. I shall send him an express. Satin and Brussels lace, but no veil. Veils are out of fashion. All the great will travel down for it. Oh, my dear Lucy. All will think it most romantic."

"Mama, all will think I *need* to get married quickly," said Lucy desperately.

Her eyes slid away from Lucy's. "Tch! You should not even consider such an idea. A band to play during the wedding breakfast. Neil Gow from Almack's, I think. I suppose we must ask some of our old friends, although people like Mrs. Belize must be content to stand outside the church and watch."

Mr. Bliss interrupted. "A word in private with you, Your Grace," he said firmly. Lucy watched them leave. Surely her father would stop this monstrous charade.

"Now, what is Mr. Bliss up to?" complained Mrs. Bliss. "It is most unlike him."

She then continued to rattle on about the wedding preparations.

"Come to my room as soon as we are free," said Lucy in a whisper to Belinda, and Belinda nodded. The duke and Mr. Bliss were absent a long time. When they eventually returned, Mr. Bliss quietly resumed his seat while Mrs. Bliss, after looking quickly from the duke to her husband, continued to plan the wedding arrangements. Any hope Lucy had of her father's stopping this hasty marriage were dashed.

She pleaded a headache and went up to her room, followed by Belinda.

"So what are you going to do?" asked Belinda.

"I do not know," said Lucy. "But I'll think of something."

"Are you determined *not* to marry the duke?" asked Belinda.

"More than ever."

"Has it crossed your mind that if you refuse to marry him, then perhaps he might be expected to marry me?" asked Belinda.

"Oh, what are we to do?" Lucy began to pace up and down the room.

"I think, Lucy, that it is time I took care of my own future," said Belinda quietly. She picked up Barney and stroked his fur. But Lucy was not listening.

The next morning the vicar, Mr. Marsham, was working in his garden, weeding a flower bed. Behind him on the lawn rolled the collie and her pups. He was wearing an old wide-awake hat to protect his head from the sun, and his oldest clothes. And then he heard the wheels of a carriage coming along the road. He prayed the carriage would go past, but it stopped at the garden gate.

He straightened up and looked over the hedge. Miss Belinda Bliss was descending from a light gig driven by one of Sarsey's grooms.

He wished he were a magician and could wave a wand over himself and transform his old clothes into his best. He snatched off his old hat and stood bowing and blushing as Belinda, with Barney at her heels, tripped into the garden. She was wearing a lacy confection of a morning gown, and her hat was a whole garden of flowers.

"Miss Belinda," he said. "I did not expect any

callers so early and . . . and . . . as you can see, I am in my old gardening clothes."

Belinda sat down on a stone bench in the garden and smiled indulgently as an ecstatic Barney tumbled forward to join his family.

"I had to see you about something," said Belinda.

"My time is yours," he said, sitting down beside her.

"I am very worried." Belinda stabbed the point of her parasol into the grass at her feet. "Yes, very worried. Wardshire has precipitated things. He is to get a special license and is to marry Lucy in three weeks time."

"He must be very much in love."

"No, I do not think so," said Belinda. "I think he is being contrary. I think he knows Lucy doesn't want him. The trouble is, if Lucy doesn't want him, Mama will make me marry him, for he more or less said that either one of us would do."

"Are you sure?"

"Oh, yes. But you do not know the whole story." Belinda told the vicar of how it was that Lucy had reported the duke to the authorities and that Lucy alone had been responsible for their arrival at that morning service, of how the duke had ruined them socially and then offered to reinstate them in the eyes of society by marriage.

"I can hardly believe it of him," said the vicar. "I know him as a very kind man, very considerate."

"I think he *might* be a little in love with Lucy," said Belinda, "but Lucy is such a clever and determined girl. She is determined he shall dislike her, and then I will not be able to marry the man of my choice."

Mr. Marsham looked bleakly about him. Only a

moment ago the sunny garden had seemed like heaven, and now it looked dark even though the sun still shone and the lilac tree above their heads sent blossoms tumbling down about them.

Barney lollopped up to them, and the vicar bent and stroked the dog's ears. "And who is the lucky gentleman of your choice?" he asked.

"You," said Belinda in a small voice.

Barney let out a yelp as the startled vicar pulled one of the dog's ears in his shock and agitation.

"I beg your pardon, Miss Belinda!"

She blushed and looked down, her long eyelashes fanned out over her cheeks.

He gingerly took one of her hands in his own.

"Did you say . . . *me*?" he asked timidly.

Belinda nodded.

"But Miss Belinda, I have very little money and . . . and . . . you are used to better things."

"Don't you want to marry me?" Belinda's soft mouth trembled.

"Oh, my heart, more than anything in the world."

"Then . . . then . . . would you be so good as to ask Papa for my hand in marriage?"

"Are you sure?"

"Yes," said Belinda demurely. She raised her eyes to his. "You may kiss me if you like."

If he liked!

It was a first kiss for both of them, clumsy, inexpert, but making the pair feel like Tristan and Isolde and Romeo and Juliet rolled into one. They kissed for a long time until Barney tugged at Belinda's gown. "I think we shall be very happy," said Belinda. "You had better get changed and come back with me."

The vicar left her in the garden and rushed indoors to look for his best suit of clothes. He felt quite sick with excitement until he remembered Mrs. Bliss, and all the happiness drained out of him. But for Belinda, he could slay dragons.

The couple were silent on the road to Sarsey. Belinda, too, was picturing her mother's rage and disappointment.

Mr. Bliss found to his bewilderment that the duke's vicar was facing him and asking for Belinda's hand in marriage. "I don't know," he said miserably. "It is all very sudden. Do you have any money other than your stipend?"

"I have three hundred a year from a family trust, sir."

"Well, it would not furnish Belinda with all the gowns and trinkets to which she has become accustomed. Also, she is very young . . ."

"We are very much in love, sir."

"And love won't wait? Well, my boy, if that is what Belinda wants, you have my blessing. But you now have her mother to cope with. You had best come with me."

The ladies were in the drawing room. The duke had just joined them, wearing riding clothes, for he had been out early on his estates.

Looking as if he were facing up to a firing squad, Mr. Bliss said in a shaky voice, "My dear, Mr. Marsham here has asked my permission to pay his addresses to Belinda, and I have given my consent."

"You what?" screamed Mrs. Bliss. "Belinda! The most beautiful girl in the county to be thrown away on a mere vicar!"

"I would remind you, madam," said the duke icily, "that Mr. Marsham is a friend of mine. I should take it as a great and personal insult if you went against his wishes."

Mrs. Bliss opened and shut her mouth like a landed pike. All at once she knew that the duke would not forgive her if she stood in his vicar's way. Why could not the duke have more exalted friends close by? Mr. Graham, for example, would have been more suitable. But she wanted this wedding for Lucy, and nothing must stand in the way of that.

"Oh, very well," she said ungraciously. "But I advise you to wait, vicar. Belinda is very young."

Belinda rose to her feet. "That's settled," she said with satisfaction. "Mr. Marsham, let us go for a walk in the garden. Come, Barney."

The butler came in at that moment to say that Farmer Jessop had called and wanted to see the duke. Lucy, not wanting to be left alone with her mother and her plans, slipped away.

She went downstairs and wandered into one of the great staterooms. She looked out of one of the windows. Belinda and her vicar were strolling arm in arm across the grass, with Barney at their heels. They were holding hands and laughing, innocence and happiness on a fine spring day.

Lucy drew back, feeling lost and bereft. With Belinda so much in love, she was left now with her own dark problem.

She walked over to the fireplace and stood with one small foot on the fender, looking down into the empty grate.

And then she heard a man's voice, quite clearly, and realized at the same time that it must be coming from a room above, the flue acting as a sound conductor.

"I was all set to marry Meg," came the man's

voice. It had a strong country burr. "But she slap my face. Now you, Your Grace, knows about the ladies. I kissed her and she slap my face and I could have swore she wanted me."

Then came the duke's voice, clear and amused. "And where were your hands, Jessop, when you were kissing her?"

"Well, I was a bit carried away, and that's a fact. I put one hand down her gown, like, for a feel."

"And Meg a virgin. Listen, Jessop, if you want to wed the girl, you will need to rein in your animal lusts until after the wedding. A virgin wants moonlight and chaste kisses and heavy sighs. Anything stronger is going to frighten her away. You must court her. Take her flowers. Lean forward and kiss her gently on the cheek. That sort of thing. The sure way to frighten any virginal female off is by mauling her and kissing her. Now, about the boundary down at the six acre . . ."

Lucy walked away from the fireplace, thinking hard. When the duke had kissed her, she had behaved surely as he had expected a virgin to behave, trembling and frightened. She was perfectly sure that if Mr. Jessop's Meg had been just as bold as he, then he might have been delighted at the time and damned her as a slut later. Such a tremendous price was laid on virginity. It was considered a young lady's most valuable asset—more valuable than her dowry or her jewels. A smile curled Lucy's lips.

What if she were to go on the attack? What if she were to kiss him passionately? Such boldness must surely disgust any man. How beautifully quiet this stateroom was! She sat down in a chair to think the matter out. The duke was getting his revenge on the Bliss family by marrying an unwilling bride. But what if she were to show herself willing? Terribly willing. The spice would surely go out of the engagement for him. He would be forced to consider what marriage to her would mean. It would mean having Mrs. Bliss in residence for most of the year.

She waited impatiently the rest of that day, but the duke was engaged in seeing his tenants and estates manager. The stationer had called on Mrs. Bliss to present his samples, and she was choosing a suitable one for the wedding invitations. "These must be ready tomorrow," she insisted, and the stationer said they would be, planning to charge her a huge sum to cover the costs of keeping his full staff at work all night long.

Lucy dressed with considerable care for dinner. Belinda came in when she had nearly finished, a radiant and happy Belinda. "You really do love your vicar," said Lucy. "And yet you barely know him."

"Yes, it is most odd," agreed Belinda. "I simply wanted someone to take me away from Mama, and he seemed so agreeable and such a lot can be done with him to make him over. He will be bishop by the time I have finished with him. But in any case, I fell in love with him, just like that."

"Oh, Belinda, leave the poor man alone. You will turn out like Mama and he will end up a bishop only because you have *nagged* him into it. Besides, bishops are very grand and do not play with dogs."

"Really?" Belinda's eyes widened.

"Yes, really, so do not ruin what you have got. Bishops are very stuffy, and the only time they ever see a dog is when they go riding to hounds."

"Papa told me this afternoon that he will make

over an allowance to me for gowns and things," said Belinda, "but I thought I could transform Mr. Marsham with it instead."

"And then he will not be the man you married. He will become like Papa, gray and scholarly and intimidated."

"I should not like that, nor should Barney," said Belinda seriously.

"And a bishop would not allow Barney to loll around on tops of beds the way he is doing on mine." As if to underline the point, Barney picked up a pillow in his teeth and proceeded to worry it with great energy until Lucy took it from him.

"But what of you?" asked Belinda. "Are you still set on getting out of the engagement?"

"More than ever, and I must be quick about it. I plan to end it before this night is out, for the stationer will have the invitations here by tomorrow, and Mama is determined to write them all out and send them by the mail coach to London."

"And what are you going to do?" asked Belinda curiously.

Lucy grinned. "I will not shock you by telling you."

"Are you ready to go downstairs, Lucy? Marsham has been invited to dinner again. Did you choose the menu?"

"Not really," said Lucy with a rueful laugh. "My plain fare did not annoy him, so I told Monsieur Pierre to have a free hand."

To Lucy's dismay, it transpired that the duke had invited several people from the county to dine, six in all, all obviously delighted at having obtained an invitation to Sarsey at last. So dinner lasted an interminable length and then the ladies retired to the drawing room, where Lucy was commanded to play for them. When the gentlemen joined them, card tables were set up, and there was a long evening of cards, followed by supper, then more cards, and it was two in the morning before the guests took their leave.

The duke's valet undressed his master for bed. The duke thought over the events of the evening. It had been pleasant to have company. Dinner had been splendid and Lucy had behaved charmingly to his guests. It was almost a pity that he was not going to marry her.

He dismissed his valet and climbed into his great four-poster bed and composed himself for sleep. He would take Lucy aside early the next day and tell her the wedding was off. He would reimburse Mrs. Bliss for the wedding invitations and that would be that.

He yawned and closed his eyes and the door opened then suddenly. There had been a soft scratching at the door. "Come in," he called. The bed curtains were drawn tightly closed. He could hear soft footsteps entering the room and assumed it was some maidservant, although he could not think of any reason why a maidservant should be in his room in the middle of the night. But the duke had long been used to being surrounded by a whole retinue of servants. Servants anticipated his every need. When he went to sit down, a footman was always there to push a chair under the ducal bottom. When his glass was nearly empty, there was always another footman to fill it. Fires were never allowed to die down and go out, or dust to lie anywhere in the great mansion.

And then the bed curtains were slowly parted and

he found that Lucy Bliss was looking down at him. "I c-came to s-say good night," she said.

"So good night, Miss Bliss," remarked the duke stonily. Lucy was in her nightdress and wrapper, with a frilly nightcap tied on her head. He suddenly wondered if she had divined that he did not want to marry her and was trying to compromise him.

"May I kiss you good night?" asked Lucy.

She really is trying to compromise me, he thought with sudden amusement. "And when I kiss you, does your mother come bursting into the room?"

Lucy gave a shudder. "No one knows I am here. You must never tell anyone! Promise!" she said fiercely.

"I promise." So she was not trying to compromise him. What was she after? The best way was surely to kiss her and then find out when she did next. He held up his arms. She stooped down and put one small hand on each shoulder and bent her mouth to his. Her mouth worked feverishly against his, more with determination than passion. He put his arms around her and lifted her onto the bed to lie beside him. "That is better," he said. He held the length of her slight body against his own and began to kiss her, but something happened to him that had not happened before. He had admitted to himself that Lucy was an attractive little thing and could rouse his senses, but now he felt hot and heavy passion surging through his veins. At first he could not get enough of kissing her, and then he wanted all of her. He freed himself from the bedclothes and rolled over on top of her.

Lucy's mind was whirling about in all this passionate blackness lit from time to time with flares of alarm. She felt cold air against her legs and realized he was raising the hem of her nightgown, and with a shriek, she jumped from the bed. "I am sorry," he said raggedly. "I do not know what came over me. I have never known such . . . Dammit, lady, do not come near my bedchamber again until we are wed."

He lay shaking long after he heard his bedroom door close. What had come over the girl? What had come over him? Oh, God, the damage was done. He would marry Lucy Bliss, mother and all, he would put up with a hundred Mrs. Blisses just to have his fill of that body, that slight, seductive body with its small, thrusting breasts and long, long legs.

After a time, he rose and splashed himself with cold water and toweled down and put on his dressing gown. He would ask Lucy, he would wake her and ask her, what had driven her to come to his bedroom.

But he stopped outside her bedroom door. He heard Belinda's voice. "I heard you crying, Lucy. What is the matter?"

He made out Lucy's voice, muffled at first as if her face were hidden in the pillow, then stronger. "I hoped to give him a disgust of me, Belinda, so I went to his bedchamber."

"Oh, no!"

"Yes, and he all but raped me."

"Lucy! That cannot be true!"

"No, no," said Lucy feverishly. "I mean he could have taken me. He is the devil, Belinda, and he knows how to take my soul away and make me want to do dreadful things like the beasts in the fields."

"But why go to him?" wailed Belinda.

"I told you. I thought my wanton behavior would

frighten him, for I have been told that gentlemen swear that no real lady is capable of passion. I hoped he might think I was not a virgin—anything to make him force me to break the engagement."

"I cannot bear to see you so unhappy," said Belinda. "Mr. Marsham likes Wardshire, so I will ask my darling to speak to the duke tomorrow, and he will listen, you'll see. Wardshire is too proud to marry anyone who doesn't want him. Perhaps instead of all these pranks and ploys, Lucy, you should just have told him. He cannot marry me now, for I am to wed Mr. Marsham. That's it! Don't you see? *Tell* him. Oh, I swear you don't know your own mind!"

Then I will make her mind up for her, thought the duke as he walked quietly away, having heard enough.

Lucy watched Belinda set out in the gig the next morning, Belinda, who was so sure she could persuade Mr. Marsham to speak to the duke. They had agreed to try that method first, and if it failed, then Lucy would simply have to face up to the duke herself.

The morning stretched out, slow hour after slow hour. Lucy discovered a great deal of Sarsey as she spent that morning avoiding the servants who had been sent by Mrs. Bliss to look for her.

At last, looking out the windows, she saw Belinda coming back and ran to meet her.

"Well?" asked Lucy eagerly.

Belinda shook her head.

"He would not do it?"

"I did not get a chance to speak to him. He had gone out driving with the duke. So I said to that dragon of a servant that I would wait. She was dreadfully grumpy but made me some tea. She kept bobbing in and telling me that she was sure the master would be away for a long time and so I should take my leave. In the end I grew impatient with her and said as I was to be Mrs. Marsham, she may as well begin by getting used to my presence in the vicarage. She threw her apron over her head and began to wail and sob and call me a scheming woman and all sorts of nasty things. She went on like a woman crossed in love, and yet she is fifty if she's a day and as ugly as sin," added Belinda with all the callousness of youth. "It was all so upsetting that I came away. I shall try to see Mr. Marsham in the afternoon, if you wish."

"No," said Lucy, "you have tried hard enough. There is no reason why I cannot break off the engagement myself, and I only wish I had thought of such a plain and sensible way of doing it before."

Belinda opened her mouth to point out that the reason Lucy had not done it before was for fear the duke might then insist on marrying her, Belinda, but was stopped from saying anything by the arrival of the duke himself, who said that he and Mr. Marsham had been to see the bishop.

That special license! Lucy said in a firm voice, "Would you be so good as to grant me an audience in private?"

"By all means," he said as Mrs. Bliss's voice could be heard from above, calling, "Lucy, is that you? Lucy, I need your help to write out these invitations."

Lucy pretended not to hear and followed the duke into the library. He kicked the logs on the hearth with one spurred and booted foot and then swung round. "What now?" he asked.

She looked up into his eyes, but they were smiling down at her in a way that made her feel weak. She looked instead at a corner table and said, "I wish to terminate our engagement. I do not want Mama to send out those invitations."

"As you will," he replied with seeming indifference. "It will have to be Belinda instead."

"It cannot be Belinda. Belinda is engaged to Mr. Marsham."

He smiled again. "Fortunately, the announcement of the engagement has not yet been sent to the newspapers. Marsham will do as I command."

"You cannot mean it."

"I do. Do you want to come with me to Mrs. Bliss and see her reaction? She always wanted Belinda to marry me, you know."

"You are a monster," raged Lucy.

"Exactly. So with your sister's happiness in mind, I suggest you look forward to your wedding. Tell me, my dear, do you usually visit gentlemen in their bedchambers?"

"Frequently," hissed Lucy. "And why should you care? You have probably kissed hundreds of females."

"Scores, I think," he corrected amiably. "Now, when I returned poor Mr. Marsham to his vicarage, he was met by his horrible servant, who was weeping and complaining about Miss Belinda, who, it transpired, had been waiting there all morning, saying she had to see the vicar, for she wanted the vicar to speak to the duke about something. What could that something have been, I wonder. Your sister is very happy and very much in love. As you are obviously very fond of her, do not do anything to distress her or dim her happiness."

Lucy looked at him silently, her mind in a turmoil. Would he really insist on Belinda marrying him if she cried off? And yet it was a risk Lucy realized that she was not prepared to take.

She found her voice. "I will make your life a misery," she vowed.

He raised her hand to his lips and kissed it. "That is more like the Lucy Bliss I know and love. You must get to know my tenants. When does your mother rise in the mornings?"

"About nine. Why?"

"Then be prepared to leave with me and go on a tour of the estate at eight tomorrow morning."

Chapter Eight

LUCY WENT INTO Belinda's bedroom very early, but her sister was fast asleep. It seemed selfish to disturb her.

She dressed herself and made her way downstairs. Four housemaids were standing together in the hall, whispering and giggling. Lucy looked at them sharply and then decided as she had no intention of ever becoming mistress of this house and staff, it did not matter a whit how the servants behaved.

A footman appeared in front of her and said the duke would like to see her in the library. Now what? thought Lucy bleakly.

The duke was seated in front of the fire. Over at a large desk by the window sat a young man, writing busily. The duke rose at Lucy's entrance, as did the young man. "My dear," said the duke, "allow me to present my most efficient secretary, Mr. Lewis. Mr. Lewis, my intended bride, Miss Bliss. Mr. Lewis will handle all the arrangements for the wedding. He knows exactly what to do. Are you ready to go out? I am anxious to introduce you to my tenants."

Lucy did not want to argue in front of the secretary. "I have to go upstairs to fetch my bonnet and cloak."

He rang the bell. "One of the servants will fetch them for you. Sit down, my dear; you should have something hot to drink." He looked over at the door as a footman entered. "Giles, be so good as to tell one of the maids to fetch a bonnet and cloak for Miss Bliss. Any preference, my dear?"

"No," said Lucy wearily, "it does not matter what I wear." The secretary looked at her in surprise.

"And bring coffee, I think, and perhaps some hot chocolate," ordered the duke.

When the servant had left, he joined Mr. Lewis at the desk and began to tick off names on a long, long list. "You will make sure all the tenants are invited, Mr. Lewis. The wedding breakfast for the guests will be indoors, and for the tenants, a marquee on the lawn just in case it rains. You will tell Mrs. Bliss, of course. Make sure too many people from London don't descend on us, for they will probably stay for weeks."

Lucy sat down by the fire and listened gloomily to all these preparations. Her heart sank even lower as she heard the duke say, "Presents have begun to arrive. Acknowledge them all." He swung round. "Would you care to see them, my dear?" Lucy shook her head. "Perhaps later," he said.

Two footmen came in carrying trays and set them down on a table in front of the fire. Lucy took a cup of coffee and some thin toast. If only there was somewhere she could run to. And then she thought of Mr. Graham. He would surely marry her and take her out of the clutches of the duke.

She raised her voice. "Is Mr. Graham traveling down from London?"

He cast her a mocking look. "I suppose so. And, alas, his fiancée."

"He is engaged?" asked Lucy, almost hearing the prison doors slam.

"Yes, and to none other than Lady Fortescue. It seemed he was disappointed in love, my dear. I had a letter from him to that effect. The lady he hoped to marry was ... er ... engaged to one of his friends, and so he took his broken heart to Lady Fortescue and they discovered they were made for each other."

So that's that, thought Lucy.

There was a tremendous bustle from the hall, and after some minutes, silence again. Then a footman appeared, followed by a maid carrying Lucy's hat and cloak. "Everything is now ready, Your Grace," he said.

What it is to be a duke, thought Lucy. All this fuss just for a morning's outing.

"Come along, Miss Bliss," said the duke. "Our carriage awaits. Mr. Lewis, I trust you will be able to manage everything."

Lucy went out into the hall. All the staff appeared to be lined up to say farewell to them. There was an air of holiday.

But a deep depression assailed her. She nodded and smiled, but barely saw anyone. She climbed in the carriage, the duke got in after her, the staff set up a cheer, and carriage and outriders moved off.

"Do you usually travel in such state, and are you usually sent on your way by cheering servants?" asked Lucy.

He settled himself comfortably in his corner and tilted his hat over his eyes. "I had very little sleep last night," he said, "so I had better get some now."

He closed his eyes and appeared to fall neatly and instantly asleep.

The carriage lurched to a stop. "Must be the lodge gates," thought Lucy. The carriage curtains were drawn tightly closed, probably because the duke did not want his sleep disturbed by the bright morning sunlight. The carriage turned in to the road and then surged forward. Lucy uttered an impatient exclamation. So tedious not to look out.

She drew back the red leather curtains on her side and blinked in the flood of bright sunlight and then blinked again in amazement. Two outriders were on her side of the carriage.

She let down the glass and leaned out. "Where are we going at this rackety pace?" she called to the outriders, but both appeared to have been struck deaf.

Panic assailed her. She took stock of her surroundings. This was a closed carriage. In her misery on leaving the hall, she had not looked at anything closely, assuming vaguely that because they were only going to visit the tenants, the duke considered a closed carriage conventional under the circumstances.

She flung herself on the sleeping duke and pummeled him awake with her fists. "What ails you?" grumbled the duke.

"This is a traveling carriage," howled Lucy. "And there are outriders."

The eyes under hooded lids looked at her sleepily and then the duke said, "Just realized it, have you?"

"We are not going to see your tenants," gasped Lucy. "Where are you taking me?"

"Gretna Green in Scotland," he said amiably. "Do let me sleep."

"Gretna . . . ? That's where people get married. At the blacksmith's. You cannot do this! Mama! Belinda! What of all the wedding arrangements?"

"I found the idea of a large wedding with hundreds of guests and your mother crowing in triumph was one that displeased me. So I decided to elope with you."

"Without even asking me?"

"You do not seem to know your own mind, my sweet, so I decided to make it up for you."

"And how am I supposed to find a clean change of clothes?"

"Your clothes are all packed and strapped on the back."

Lucy remembered the giggling housemaids and realized that they must have been waiting for her to descend and go into the library so that they could pack her things.

"You are out to ruin me!" she cried.

"Not I. You will be described as my cousin at each posting house. I do mean to marry you."

"And make Mama's humiliation complete?"

"Oh, Mrs. Bliss may have her wedding. Belinda will be married, not you. I persuaded the vicar to get a special license from his bishop. I will foot the bill, and Monsieur Farré may design a gown for Belinda."

"You had it all planned," said Lucy. "But you will not succeed. I will run away!"

"Where? Back to Mrs. Bliss to tell her you don't want a duke after all? Now, be a good girl and cease pestering me. I plan to sleep until the first stop."

Lucy sat in a turmoil of fury. She clasped her

hands together tightly. Panicking would not help. Somehow she must hit on a way to escape from him.

Never had the servants at Sarsey witnessed such a scene when Mrs. Bliss found the duke had escaped her. Mr. Lewis, the secretary, stood quietly before her. He had explained matters to her and was now glad the duke had warned him of what he would have to endure. But he had been promised extra payment for coping with such as Mrs. Bliss, and so he decided to wait until this formidable matron's hysterics were over.

It was almost as if Mrs. Bliss suddenly remembered she had a husband. She tugged the bell and demanded that Mr. Bliss present himself in the drawing room immediately.

"I shall sue him for breach of promise," panted Mrs. Bliss, meaning the duke.

"You can hardly do that, madam," pointed out Mr. Lewis. "His Grace *is* going to marry your daughter."

"He has ruined me, you nincompoop," shouted Mrs. Bliss.

"Hardly," said Mr. Lewis, deliberately misunderstanding her. "For the wedding is to go ahead, but between Miss Belinda and Mr. Marsham, and His Grace has said he will pay for everything."

Mr. Bliss entered the room quietly and stood looking at them.

"Mr. Bliss!" cried his wife. "But hear this! Wardshire has eloped to Gretna with Lucy!"

"Yes. I know," said Mr. Bliss. "His Grace informed me of his plans."

Mrs. Bliss turned puce. "And you did not tell me?"

"We discussed the matter and came to the conclusion it was better not to."

"Your own wife? Why?"

"Because you would have inflicted a hellish scene on Lucy, and I think she has enough to bear. I am convinced after all that Wardshire will make her a good husband. I think perhaps that Lucy might be a little in love with him."

"How could you? How *dare* you? Oh, all the people that have been invited!"

"They will find themselves at Belinda's wedding instead. Mr. Lewis says he will take the blame and say he put the wrong name on the invitations, which is handsome of him. He will also handle the arranging of everything. Belinda is a very lucky girl."

Mrs. Bliss struck her bosom dramatically. "You have betrayed me, Mr. Bliss. I will have nothing to do with this farce of a wedding. Oh, when I think of the grand guests, all coming to find out my daughter is wedding a common vicar."

"Belinda is marrying a fine young man. You should be happy for her. You have had your way long enough, Mrs. Bliss. I am going off with Mr. Lewis to discuss the arrangements, and I suggest you leave it to us."

At that moment Belinda entered the room. Mrs. Bliss started up again at the sight of her, and Mr. Bliss and Mr. Lewis took the opportunity to make their escape.

Belinda listened solemnly to her mother's lamentations, and when Mrs. Bliss had finally talked herself dry, Belinda said, "Well, I think that is handsome of Wardshire. I must go to see Mr. Marsham."

"You could have married a title," said Mrs. Bliss bitterly. "You are an ungrateful girl, as bad as your father. I have a headache. I am going to my room and do not wish to be disturbed."

"I do not think anyone would want to," remarked Belinda to her mother's retreating back.

But when she was left alone, Belinda began to worry about Lucy and how she was faring. She was also worried that Mr. Marsham had said nothing about it to her.

Some minutes later she descended to the hall, dressed to go out, and asked a footman to fetch the gig from the stables.

Mr. Marsham was working on his sermon when his beloved was ushered by his dragon of a maid, who threw Belinda a venomous look before leaving the room.

"I do not think your maid is ever going to like me," sighed Belinda.

"You must not worry yourself over her," said Mr. Marsham. "I found another position for her. She will be replaced by a cheerful young girl from the village."

"All these arrangements going on behind my back," mourned Belinda. "And poor Lucy being dragged off to Scotland! You might have told me."

"I would have done, my love," said Mr. Marsham, "if His Grace had not sworn me to secrecy. So we are to be married in quite a rush. Do you mind so very much?"

"Oh, no. May we keep *all* the dogs?"

"As many as you like," said the doting vicar.

Belinda smiled sunnily. "Well, in that case, I forgive you all. But poor Lucy . . ."

He gathered her in his arms and began to kiss

her, and Belinda forgot all about her sister for the moment and kissed him back with great enthusiasm while Barney sat at their feet and looked up at them curiously for a few moments before going in search of his family.

It had been a long, weary day for Lucy. She refused to talk to the duke. They finally stopped for the night at a town with the depressing name of Puddledyke. Lucy endured dinner in a private parlor with the duke, who talked lightly of this and that and seemed amused by her taciturn silence. But her anger was mixed with fear. They had adjoining bedchambers. What if he planned to share her bed?

But the duke merely suggested at the end of the meal that she might like to retire early and said he would send a maid to help her unpack and she would be called at six in the morning.

Lucy was glad to escape from him. With him, she felt overshadowed by his personality and unable to think clearly about what to do.

She instructed the maid to take out her nightrail, a traveling gown, and a change of linen, but to leave everything else as it was. No point in unpacking any more when she had to leave in the morning.

While the maid was stooping to put more logs on the fire, Lucy, watching her, suddenly remembered a lecture she had heard given by a mannish woman called Miss Tibbs. Miss Tibbs had given a lecture in the town hall near Lucy's home about two years ago about women's rights. She had said that it was shameful that so many women should become the slaves of men because there was no other option open to them. She urged them to consider that it was possible to break class bounds to obtain freedom. One could always become a servant. This had produced a shocked murmur from the ladies in her audience. But Lucy remembered those words now.

"Is there a large house near here?" she asked.

The maid turned round and bobbed a curtsy. "There be Sir George Clapham. Two Trees, his house is called. 'Bout a mile out on the west road."

'Thank you. Pray see that I am not disturbed in the morning." The maid curtsied again and left.

Lucy searched her luggage and found to her delight that the maids had packed her traveling writing case. She sat down and wrote two references for herself, sanded them, and put them into her reticule. She knew she had ten guineas and some silver in her purse, more than enough for her purpose.

She waited until two in the morning and then packed a few items in a bandbox, swung a heavy cloak about her shoulders, and made her way downstairs. The inn was still coping with arriving and departing travelers. She walked through the inn yard and out into the town. She stopped a watchman and asked him for the inn where the stagecoaches called, and was told it was the Goat and Compasses, about ten minutes walk away.

She presented herself at the coaching inn, knowing she had made a good choice. Unlike the elegant posting house, it had a more anonymous air. To her relief, she was able to obtain a room. She used the name Miss Tibbs, paid her shot in advance, and said she did not want to be disturbed early in the morning as she planned to sleep late.

In the morning, keeping to the shadows of the buildings and looking about her from time to time for fear of being discovered by the duke's servants, she found a secondhand clothes shop and purchased two black gowns, two print gowns, three aprons, and three caps.

Satisfied, she returned to the inn and ordered a hearty breakfast to be sent up to her room. She felt happier than she had done for a long time. She felt in control of her destiny. She packed her new clothes into the bandbox and quietly left the inn and walked the half mile out of town to Two Trees, Sir George Clapham's home.

After the intimidating grandeur of Sarsey, it looked to Lucy like a relatively modest manor. It was an old house, and so the servants' quarters were to the side of the house, the rustic as it was called, rather than being in the basement.

She knocked loudly at the kitchen door, and it was answered by an off-duty footman in his shirt-sleeves. "I am looking for employment," said Lucy bluntly.

"Better come in," said the footman. He led the way through the scullery and kitchen to the servants' hall. "Wait there," he said, "and I'll get Mrs. Foxe."

After about ten minutes, Mrs. Foxe, the housekeeper, appeared, great cap nodding, keys jangling. She was a small, squat woman with a yellowish complexion and a great wide mouth and bulging eyes. Lucy thought she looked like a toad.

"What d'ye want, girl?" demanded Mrs. Foxe.

"I am looking for employment," said Lucy, coarsening her vowels.

"Where did you come from?"

"Off the stage from London, madam."

"Why? Why Puddledyke?"

Lucy hung her head. "Come on, out with it," snapped Mrs. Foxe. "Some fellow, was it?"

"Yes, madam," whispered Lucy. "A soldier. He said he lived here and that he would marry me, but I went to the address he gave me and there isn't such a place."

"Are you with child?"

"Oh, no, madam."

"Name?"

"Lucy Tibbs."

"References?"

Lucy produced her forged references and held them out.

"You've worked in two grand London households," commented the housekeeper. Lucy was particularly proud of the reference she had written for herself from Lady Fortescue. "Your cloak is of merino wool and your shoes are of the finest leather."

"Lady Fortescue was fond of me," said Lucy, manufacturing a dismal sniff. "I never should have left her. She let me have some of her old clothes."

Mrs. Foxe studied Lucy in silence for what seemed an age. Then she said, "By chance, I need a housemaid. Betty was six months gone and so we had to get rid of her. Wait here. I'll need to consult the mistress."

When she had gone, Lucy sagged in her chair with sudden weariness. To bolster her spirits, she reminded herself fiercely that she had only to hide out for as long as it would take the duke to forget about her.

Mrs. Foxe eventually returned and said, "Follow me."

Lucy followed along a stone-flagged passage, then

through a small, square hall and up polished oaken stairs to a drawing room above.

Lady Clapham was reclining on a chaise longue by the window.

Lucy curtsied low before her. She was later to learn that Lady Clapham was a professional invalid. She was a large, fat woman with a doughy face and a petulant mouth.

"This here is Lucy Tibbs," said the housekeeper.

"Take off your bonnet, girl," ordered Lady Clapham. Lucy untied the strings of her bonnet and took it off. "She's quite pretty," said Lady Clapham.

"But too slight," commented Mrs. Foxe.

"Yes, you have the right of it. He likes them buxom. I think you will do. That business with Betty was more than enough. Take her away, Mrs. Foxe, and explain her wages and duties to her."

Lucy's position was to be that of under housemaid. She was told of the pittance she would earn and then turned over to the upper housemaid, a cheerful Irish girl called Mary.

Lucy was to start work immediately on Lady Clapham's bedchamber, and her query "Is not that the duty of the chambermaid?" brought the reply that it was not a grand London household and she had better not give herself airs. Lucy was glad she was supervised by Mary. She had not realized there was so much work in cleaning a bedroom.

First the bed was stripped, and then she had to brush the mattress. Once the bed was made, she had to shake the bedcurtains, lay them smoothly on the bed, pinning up the bottom valances so that she could dust underneath. Then she unlooped the window curtains, shook them, and pinned them up out of the way. Next the room had to be cleared of all ornaments, which were carried down to the kitchen to be washed. Returning to the bedroom, she spread a dust sheet on the bed. The toilet covers were then shaken and placed on the bed. Next came the work of cleaning the carpet. This was first sprinkled with squeezed tea leaves and cut grass and then swept thoroughly. After the grate was polished, she then washed the toilet table, water jugs, water bottles, and tumblers with a mixture of soap and hot water and soda.

The boards of the floor left bare by the carpet then were scrubbed white with soda and water. Then everything else was polished and dusted, and the ornaments washed and put back before the curtains could be unpinned and the toilet cloths replaced.

While she worked, Mary talked. "You'll have to be careful of the master," she said. "Sure, he's a devil with the girls. He got poor Betty in the family way."

"Did he rape her?" asked Lucy.

"No, just turned the silly girl's head with flattery and presents. Pity. I liked Betty. You'll be after wanting to know who's here. Well, there meself, and then there's the footman, James, and there's Mrs. Foxe, the butler, Mr. Jones, the scullery maid, Jenny, the odd man, Binks, and a betweenstairs maid, Josie. The page, Jem, does the pots and knives and helps the outdoor staff when he's not running errands. And of course, the cook, Mrs. Greenaway. We're a pretty happy lot. If you start at six in the morning, you can get through enough work to have an hour off in the afternoon. You work hard and you look clean, but where did you get hands like that?"

Mary looked down in amazement at the soft white skin of Lucy's mall hands.

"My last employer let me wear gloves the whole time," said Lucy.

"Well, that's London for you, I s'pose."

Lucy worked diligently all that day. There seemed to be no end to the tasks she had to do, from trimming the lamps and cleaning the candlesticks to dusting all the books in the library with a goose feather.

Then the evening finally arrived. The bedroom windows had to be opened before sunset and then firmly closed two hours later. Nightclothes to be laid out, beds to be turned down, fires to be made up, and back to the kitchen to use the crumb brush on the dinner napkins and then fold them into their proper rings along with a myriad of other jobs. Lucy volunteered the knowledge that in some households, meaning her own, napkins were washed every time they became dirty, and the other servants looked at her in amazement, for nothing in the Clapham household was washed until laundry day. Even the tablecloth was simply put into the linen press each evening and then returned to the table the following day.

When Lucy eventually climbed into the bed she was to share with Mary and the betweenstairs maid, she felt exhausted. The satanic face of the Duke of Wardshire danced before her eyes before she plunged down into a dreamless sleep.

The Duke of Wardshire was a very angry man. He had checked at every livery stable and coaching office, but no one answering the description of Lucy Bliss had appeared at any of them. He had ridden out along the roads leading from the town in case she had been mad enough to go on foot, his servants searched high and low, but there was no sign of Lucy Bliss.

One day passed, and then another. He was about to go to the authorities and start a full-scale search of the town and countryside with all the help he could muster when he was told by one of his footmen that he had two callers.

"Who the devil are they?" snapped the duke, who was preparing to go out again on another search.

"A Sir George and Lady Clapham."

"Never heard of them. Send them to the right-about. How did they know I was here anyway?"

"There is a paragraph in this morning's local paper," said the footman. "Sir George is a local worthy."

"I don't care if he's the king of England."

"Beg pardon, Your Grace," said the footman, "but this Sir George will know the town and country. Perhaps a few discreet inquiries about Miss Bliss . . . ?"

"You're right. Show them up."

Lady Clapham, roused from her "sickbed" by the prospect of meeting a duke, gushed in, followed by her husband. The duke immediately found them uncongenial and tiresome. They were not the sort of people he could ask about Lucy Bliss. He completed his toilet with his back to them, barely hearing Lady Clapham's voice because she was babbling on about the servant problem.

"But we have just engaged a very superior girl.

She was formerly with Lady Fortescue's household. Do you know Lady Fortescue?"

"I beg your pardon." The duke swung round and gave an irritated tug at his cuff.

"I was just saying, Your Grace, that we have lately engaged a very superior sort of girl who used to be in Lady Fortescue's household. Are you acquainted with her?"

"Your servant?"

Sir George gave a beefy laugh. "How could you know our Lucy? No, my wife meant Lady Fortescue."

"Yes, I do know her," said the duke slowly. "Did you say Lucy?"

"Our new housemaid, yes."

She wouldn't, he thought. She couldn't . . . Aloud he said, "There was some talk about a servant of Lady Fortescue. Describe this girl."

Lady Clapham leaned forward. "Lucy Tibbs? Small, slight girl."

"Large gray eyes?" asked the duke impatiently. "Good clothes?"

"She arrived in good clothes, yes. She said Lady Fortescue had given them to her."

The duke smiled slowly. "I regret to inform you, Lady Clapham, that your new maid was dismissed from Lady Fortescue's household for theft."

"I'll send her to the constable," growled Sir George.

"Do not do that," said the duke, "as a favor to me. Lady Fortescue told me the girl was of a fairly good family but fallen on hard times. It will be punishment enough if you dismiss her. Now, if you will excuse me . . . ?"

He then spent the next five minutes in slowly

propelling them to the door of his room while he declined all the invitations that were being showered down on him, from turtle dinners to musicales.

Having finally got rid of them, he rang the bell and ordered his carriage to be made ready. Now for Miss Lucy Bliss!

Chapter Nine

DESPITE HER FATIGUE, Lucy was beginning to enjoy herself. The hard work kept thought at bay. She felt secure. The duke would have long since given her up and gone back to Sarsey. She had a nagging fear, certainly, that he might decide to revenge himself on the Bliss family by marrying Belinda, but a voice in her head told her he would never hurt his vicar, or Belinda for that matter, and it showed the extent of her tiredness in that she did not consider this perception of a new and kinder duke at all strange.

While Sir George and his lady were visiting the duke, although the servants did not know where they had gone, only that they had gone to pay a call on someone in the town, the staff decided to relax and take a break. It was not often that both the Claphams were absent, Lady Clapham preferring to lie at her ease surrounded by patent medicines and act the invalid.

The cook produced a batch of hot scones and an enormous pot of tea. There was a lot of chatter and banter around the table in the servants' hall. One could never be lonely as a servant, thought Lucy. They were all bound together against their employers, a small army of slaves taking their comfort where and when they could.

"Demme, that was short," groaned the butler as the sound of carriage wheels coming up the drive reached their ears through the open window of the servants' hall. He pulled on his coat, as did the footman, and both then ran through to the hall.

Stretching and complaining, the other servants rose from the table to go about their duties. But the butler was soon back. "Mrs. Foxe," he said, "they are in a rare taking. Lady Clapham wants to see you immediately."

Mrs. Foxe waddled to the door. "Now what's the matter?" she grumbled. "Everything's clean downstairs."

Lucy collected her box of black lead and brushes and prepared to follow Mary up to the bedchambers to start cleaning the fireplaces. Mary was searching for her favorite feather duster while Lucy stood waiting for her when Mrs. Foxe came back.

"Lucy Tibbs," said the housekeeper, "pack your things this minute and get out of this house. We don't want no thieves here."

"What is this?" demanded Lucy. "I am no thief!"

"Don't dare argify. Get out!" shouted Mrs. Foxe.

Lucy looked wildly around at the other servants for support, but they all avoided her gaze. There was no way she could demand to be taken to Lady Clapham and plead her innocence. There was no way she could protest she was a liar and forger but not a thief. The fatigue that had been so comfortable in a way now left her shaken and trembling and hardly capable of coping with this new shock.

She went sadly up to the maids' room to collect her things, humiliated by the fact that Mary followed her up— "to make sure you don't pinch anything o' mine."

Her few things put away quickly in the bandbox, she held out her hand to Mary. "I am not a thief," said Lucy quietly. "Please believe me." But Mary ignored her hand and turned away.

Blinking away tears, Lucy went down, through the servants' hall and the kitchen and so out through the side door. Her bandbox banging against her legs, she trudged wearily down the drive.

At the lodge gates she stopped abruptly. The duke's carriage stood there, with the duke himself beside it. Lucy was too tired to even think of escaping. He held open the carriage door. She climbed in. He got in after her. His footman put up the steps and then the carriage dipped and swayed as he jumped on the backstrap.

Mary stood behind a slim oak tree and watched openmouthed. It had suddenly struck her that this Lucy Tibbs could not be a thief and she wasn't going to believe it, no matter what anyone said, and so she had run after Lucy to tell her so and to wish her luck. She watched in amazement until the carriage had disappeared and then ran back to the house and dashed into the servants' hall, crying out that Lucy had been taken up by a lord and swept off in his carriage. It was a grand lord, for she had seen a crest on the carriage and there were outriders and everything. For a long time to come, the servants were to mull over the strangeness of Lucy Tibbs, most coming to the conclusion that she had been this lord's mistress and had run away from him. Mary volunteered that she thought Lucy was a real lady after all, and the grand lord had probably been a member of her family, but she was howled down. Who had ever heard of a lady working as hard as Lucy Tibbs?

"Go to sleep," ordered the Duke of Wardshire. "You look exhausted. We will talk later."

Too shaken and tired to argue and not wanting to talk to him, Lucy obediently closed her eyes. She did not expect to fall asleep, but fall asleep she did.

The duke watched her as she slept. The game was no longer amusing him. He could have coped with a raging and furious Lucy, not this exhausted little girl with the wide, hurt eyes and violet shadows under them. He would have to marry her now, whether she wanted him or not. And he had begun to think she really wanted him. But that was before she had run away to become a servant. He could not keep the elopement quiet. Mrs. Bliss would have told too many people about it by now. He should have brought some respectable female along as chaperone. That way he could have given her the freedom she now so obviously craved.

Lucy slept heavily. There was a smear of black lead on her face. She must really loathe and fear him to have stooped to become a servant. And he had thought it all a game and that, yes, she would come to love him. When had he first begun to love Lucy Bliss? Perhaps on the very first day when he had seen her with that dreadful mother of hers.

He became hungry, but he did not want to disturb her and so the carriage sped on, stopping only to change the horses.

At last at four in the afternoon, Lucy murmured something and stirred and then her eyes flew open. "Do not be alarmed," he said quietly. "I am not going to berate you. We will talk after we have dined."

Lucy nodded dumbly. The coach stopped at a posting house somewhere on the outskirts of Carlisle. Despite her misery, Lucy felt comforted by the sight of the large, well-appointed bedchamber and by the quiet deftness of the housemaids who had been sent up to unpack her clothes. She was told that the duke had ordered dinner to be served in a private parlor at six o'clock and so asked for a bath to be carried up and scrubbed herself in front of the fire until she had removed all the traces of black lead from under her fingernails and everywhere else it had managed to stick. Black lead was dreadful stuff, mused Lucy. It got everywhere. She tried to think of her fellow servants, but their faces were now small and distant in her mind.

She felt much more like her courageous and battling self when she eventually presented herself in the parlor with freshly washed hair and wearing one of her prettiest muslin gowns. She realized she was very hungry indeed and concentrated on eating, ignoring the duke, wondering what he would say.

When the cover was cleared and fruit and nuts and decanters were put on the polished surface of the table, he began to talk. "I am not going to blame you for running away," he said in a level voice.

Lucy sat very still, startled by the gravity of his voice.

"It all started out so badly." He sighed. "It seemed a joke. You see, my dear, it could not until now occur to me that anyone would not want to marry me. Arrogant? Despite the evil reputation I built up for myself, I have been pursued quite dreadfully. I therefore thought that your protests were of little account. I am used to my own way in everything." He paused and refilled her glass and then his own. "So," he went on in a measured voice, "it took your running away to become a servant to bring me to my senses.

"But we are trapped, you and I. To return unwed would mean ruin for you. So we must go through with it. But I will repay you. After we are married and returned to Sarsey, we will make all the necessary arrangements. You may live your own life, my wife in name only. You may live where you please and consider yourself free. I would only beg of you that if you decide to take a lover, be discreet about it. I will settle a handsome income on you. You will want for nothing."

Lucy sat looking at him in amazement. "I surprise you?" he mocked with something of his old manner. "The wicked duke shocks you? Perhaps you think it is another trick, but I assure you I speak the truth. We will continue to Gretna and go through with this farce of a marriage. Do you agree?"

Her thoughts were in a whirl. She had longed for a means of escape from her mother, and now he was handing such an escape to her on a plate. But then one thought as clear as a bell chimed through the rest—he does not love me. If he loved me, he would want me, not as a wife in name only. But why should that matter so very much?

"I await your answer," he said gently.

She put a hand to her head. "I am still tired. I cannot think clearly. Was it you who told Sir George and Lady Clapham that I was a thief?"

"I am afraid so. They came to call on me, and

Lady Clapham in the manner of that type of woman started talking about her servants and mentioned a Lucy."

"I was a good servant," said Lucy quietly. "I found the work dreadfully hard, but it gave me a feeling of courage and independence to be earning my bread. Do you understand?"

"Yes, I think I can."

She rubbed her nose in distress. "As you say, we are both trapped and you have given me a generous offer. May I give you my reply in the morning?"

"By all means." He stood up and went to draw her chair back for her as she rose as well. He kissed her lightly on the check, a peck of a kiss, and said good night, a goodnight that Lucy echoed in a sad little voice.

She did not go to bed but sat by the fire, staring into the flames, a bit of her mind appreciating the luxury of a fire at a time of year when more common inns would have ceased to light them. She tried to sort out her jumbled thoughts, to be honest with herself. What had piqued her about the duke, she realized with a sigh, was that he had never professed to love her, and that was what had hurt her pride. Somewhere in the back of her mind when she had run away to be a servant had been the romantic thought that he *would* find her at last and say he loved her. She could not be married to such a man without his love. He had mentioned she might take a lover. How would *she* feel if he took a mistress? A sudden stab of sick jealousy supplied that answer. And so she had probably been in love with him all along but had stubbornly refused to acknowledge it.

And yet what could she do? And then slowly she

began to think she had hit on the answer, on a possible solution. If she managed to stay away for a few weeks, then Belinda would be safely married. She had enough money left to buy herself a seat on the outside of a stagecoach. All she had to do was to find another position as a servant. She still had those forged references. She would need all her courage to go out into this strange northern town and find work. Then after a few weeks she would travel south and seek refuge with Belinda. She could never marry now. Belinda would not turn her out. Now that she knew the duke a little better, she did not anticipate any trouble from him. He had looked so . . . sad. He would be relieved to be shot of her.

She set the clock in her mind for five in the morning. But first she must leave a letter for the duke.

It took almost an hour for her to complete the short letter. In it she told him she was as much to blame as he, that she had in her way goaded him into this action. He must not marry someone he did not love. That, she had realized, would be a dreadful tragedy, wrote Lucy. She herself could not live with someone who did not love her. She begged him to forgive her and not to try to find her.

Then she sanded and sealed the letter with a slight feeling of relief. She packed her servants' clothes into that bandbox and then went to bed for a few hours sleep.

The early morning light, dull and gray, suited her mood as she crept from the posting house. As it was only a short way out of town, she had hopes of seeing the gates of some mansion on her road.

Soon she could see the gray buildings of Carlisle in front of her in the morning haze. And then on her right she noticed a lodge house and two tall gates topped with stone griffins.

Anxious not to annoy the gatekeeper by waking him so early, she climbed over the wall and then made her way up a long drive. She was wearily wondering if in fact it led anywhere at all when she rounded a bend and saw a large stone house in front of her. It had a comfortable air of prosperity. Smoke was rising from several of the chimneys.

Lucy made her way around the side of the house, wondering now whether she could expect to be lucky again. Neither her mother nor her mother's friends would dream of hiring an itinerant housemaid for one moment.

She heard a clatter of dishes from the basement and went down some stone steps to a stout door with a bell on a rope beside it. She rang the bell, hoping the servants were all awake.

The door was answered by an urchin, coatless and in his bare feet. Lucy asked to speak to the housekeeper and was told to walk inside. Another servants' hall, another row of curious faces. There appeared to be a large number of servants. The housekeeper rose and came to stand before her. She was a thin, gaunt woman with a harsh face.

"Come with me," she said, and led the way up the backstairs to her parlor on the half landing.

"I am Mrs. Moreton," she said. "State your business."

"I am looking for employ," whispered Lucy, feeling intimidated.

"As is every felon on the north road. In what capacity?"

"As housemaid, an it please you, ma'am." Lucy dropped a curtsy.

"Well, go on," said Mrs. Moreton. "He tricked you, didn't he? Went back to his regiment, did he?"

Lucy thanked all the men of the British army for their notorious unfaithfulness. To tell a good lie, she had to mostly believe it herself, so she threw her heart into her story. But as she talked of her love for this mythical soldier, she thought of the duke, and as she thought of him, tears welled up in her eyes and spilled down her cheeks.

"I thought so," said Mrs. Moreton. "Men were ever thus. Fiends all of them. The master, Mr. Camden, is not married and so he gives me a free hand with the girls. I shall put you on trial. If you do your work well, I shall keep you. If you slack or slouch for one minute, then you will be sent on your way."

Lucy scrubbed her eyes dry and then searched in her reticule. "My references," she said.

"Pooh! My own eyes are my references. Girls can have all sorts of references and yet be slack at their work. Mr. Camden is entertaining a party of house-guests and so I could do with an extra pair of hands. You have your uniform?"

"Yes, ma'am."

"I will show you your room. Get changed and present yourself in the servants' hall as quickly as possible."

As Lucy changed into her print gown and tied on her cap and apron, she relished the idea of the hard work to come. She did not mind slaving now. All she wanted to do was blot any memory of the Duke of Wardshire from her mind.

The duke's servants had never seen him in such a rage as he was that morning when he awoke and found Lucy Bliss had fled. He had been generous towards her, he had treated her with courtesy and kindness, and this was how she repaid him. He had thrown open the windows of his room in the morning, and the fresh breeze that had blown in had lifted the letter from Lucy, which she had slid under his door, and deposited it behind the coal scuttle. So the duke was left to think she had simply run off again without having the decency to let him know.

He told his servants that he would search for her himself. First he asked the landlord for the address of the nearest large house, and having been told it was Bramley, home of a Mr. Camden, he rode there, bitterness in his heart. He demanded to see Mr. Camden and was ushered up to that gentleman's bedchamber.

Mr. Camden was a white-haired, jolly-looking man, already propped up against his pillows when the duke arrived and interested to learn what had brought the great duke calling on him.

The duke realized quickly that this was someone he could trust, and so he told the fascinated Mr. Camden all about his engagement to Lucy Bliss and their adventures. "So the blunt fact is, sir," said the duke, "that Miss Bliss prefers the life of a servant to that of my wife."

"Amazing," said Mr. Camden, shaking his head in amazement. "Probably totty-headed. Got inbreeding in the Bliss family?"

Despite his anger, the duke smiled. "Not that I know of, but I am become doubtful of my own sanity. Would you be so good, sir, to ask if a housemaid called Lucy—she will keep her first name, I am sure—has been engaged this morning without making it look as if it is any concern of mine?"

"Gladly." Mr. Camden rang the bell beside the bed. "We'll have Mrs. Moreton in here. Looks like a dragon of a woman but got a soft heart. Might have engaged a girl on the doorstep if she was spun a hard-luck story."

A footman came in and was told to fetch the housekeeper. The duke waited impatiently, persuading himself that he only wanted to know she was safe.

Mrs. Moreton entered and stood waiting. "Ah, Mrs. Moreton," said Mr. Camden. "This gentleman is writing a scholarly treatise on servants' conditions in England."

The duke blinked.

"So," went on Mr. Camden, who was enjoying himself immensely, "perhaps you can tell him about conditions here."

The duke fretted while Mrs. Moreton, looking all the while at him as if she thought it an odd occupation for a gentleman, outlined the number of staff, the wages, holidays allowed, sleeping accommodation, and the state of the kitchens.

"Taken on anyone new?" asked Mr. Camden when she had finished.

"A new housemaid. This morning. She's on trial."

"Where did she come from?"

"Just turned up, Usual story. Tricked by a soldier. You know, sir, these fiends promise the girls marriage and then go back to their regiments."

"And this Mary Jane or whatever her name is . . ."

"Lucy, sir."

"Ah, Lucy. Yes, strong, sturdy type?"

"No, sir, very slight but wiry. I think she will do. Pretty manners, and that's rare enough these days."

"Thank you, Mrs. Moreton, that will be all."

When the housekeeper had left, Mr. Camden looked at the duke with the bright inquisitiveness of a robin. "What would you like me to do?"

"She is safe here," said the duke bitterly. "If that is what she wants, let her have it. Should she become ill or show any signs of leaving, inform me by express. I shall, however, have to inform her parents where she is, and they will probably come and fetch her. In the meanwhile, please do not let anyone know of my interest in her."

Lucy heard that evening of the duke's visit, for although his name had not been given to Mrs. Moreton, the butler who had announced him was eager to tell them all about how the duke had looked and what he had worn, and for one glorious moment her heart surged with hope. He would take her away, he would say he loved her.

But that hope died as Mrs. Moreton began to complain that dukes ought to behave like dukes and not go writing things about servants.

"Did he ask for the names of the staff here?" asked Lucy anxiously.

"Didn't ask anything. Mr. Camden, he did all the asking. Asked me if we have taken anyone on recently, and I said only you."

So the duke knew she was here, thought Lucy, and yet had gone away. That was that. She had wanted so many times to make him disgusted with her, and now she had succeeded. And when she eventually left to go to stay with Belinda, she would be near Sarsey and with the vicar, and the duke could order the vicar to turn her out. She would need to go back to her mother and endure a lifetime of recrimination.

It took the duke less than two days to return to Sarsey. He found his home full of guests and bustling with preparations for Belinda's wedding. He went to the library and asked Mr. and Mrs. Bliss and Belinda and Mr. Marsham to be sent to him.

Mr. Marsham had been visiting Belinda, so soon all were present and demanding to know where Lucy was.

"She has run away from me," said the duke harshly. "She is working as a housemaid."

Mrs. Bliss turned pale. "You must be funning. A daughter of mine as a servant! And you have not married her? And yet she has been with you."

Mr. Bliss said coldly, "Please explain carefully what happened, Your Grace."

And so the duke told them as best as he could. He said that he and Mrs. Bliss between them had driven Lucy into servitude as she could not bear the idea of being married to him, nor could she obviously bear returning to her mother.

Belinda began to cry, and Mr. Marsham comforted her.

Mrs. Bliss found her voice. "The shame of it," she wailed. "Have I not had enough to bear with the guests here wondering why it is Belinda who is wedding a vicar and not a duke wedding Lucy? And they do not like the idea that the grand wedding gifts they sent or brought should go to such an undistinguished pair."

"What are you going to do about your daughter?" demanded the duke.

"I am casting her off," panted Mrs. Bliss. "She may be ruined, but she is not going to ruin me. All my friends will be at the wedding."

"Then I will go for her," cried Belinda.

"No," said Mr. Bliss quietly. "I will fetch her. All is not lost. No one but your servants and ourselves know you went off with Lucy to Gretna Green. I have made sure Mrs. Bliss told nobody. If you constrain your servants to silence, Your Grace, then Lucy's reputation can be saved."

"You may take my traveling carriage and servants," said the duke. "I will come with you."

"No," said Mr. Bliss sadly. "You had better let me go alone. It is only a few days to Belinda's wedding. With any luck, we will be back by then."

"I have her belongings with me," said the duke.

"She left all her clothes!" screamed Mrs. Bliss.

"Servants do not need much," said the duke. "Mr. Bliss, I suggest you set out tomorrow at first light."

In the posting house outside Carlisle, a maidservant found Lucy's letter behind the coal scuttle half an hour after the duke had left. She gave it to the landlord. The landlord, anxious to impress so important a client as the Duke of Wardshire, rode into the Royal Mail office in Carlisle and paid for the letter's postage.

The letter reached the nearest large town to Sarsey, Barminster, where it was decided to send a post boy out with it to the duke, rather than keeping it to go out with the usual bag in the morning.

And so it was that the duke, immured in his library and refusing to see any of his guests, was disturbed late at night by his secretary, who handed him Lucy's letter, wrapped round which was a covering letter from the landlord to say that it had been found shortly after the duke's departure.

More recriminations, he thought wearily as he broke open the seal. He read and reread the letter. A warm glow started up somewhere inside him. It was all so very simple. She did not want a loveless marriage, and fool that he was, he had never told her he loved her.

He went in search of Mr. Bliss, finally having to enlist his servants to help him find him. Mr. Bliss had become expert at hiding from his wife and was finally found out in one of the succession houses, sitting among the plants, reading a book.

Silently the duke showed him the letter, and Mr. Bliss's face brightened. "So may I suggest," he said, "that you go yourself?"

"Immediately," said the duke with a grin.

"And will you be back in time for Belinda's wedding, or do you still plan to go to Gretna?"

"I still have that special license," said the duke, "and if she will have me, then it will be a double wedding."

He then went in search of his secretary and told Mr. Lewis to make preparations for a double wedding and to inform the bishop, and the overworked Mr. Lewis bit back a groan. It was understood that Mrs. Bliss should know nothing of his plans. The servants were to be gathered together and told again that they must not breathe a word of his journey to Gretna with Miss Bliss. Then the grooms and coachman and footmen who had been relaxing after the grueling journey south were told to make ready to go back again.

All the long journey, the duke saw Lucy's face dancing before his tired eyes. What if he told her he loved her and that did not do the trick? But he would bring her home anyway. Horses were changed, posting houses came and went, the fatigued servants swore and grumbled as the carriage hurtled over northwards, the duke answering their grumbles by saying that if the mail coach could travel from London to Edinburgh in thirty-four and a half hours, then they could make it to Carlisle in considerably less time.

Chapter Ten

LUCY HAD FOUND the work at Sir George Clapham's very hard, but the work at Mr. Camden's was double because of the house party.

His guests were all gentlemen, a fishing party, noisy, often drunk, often muddy, and ever-demanding. Bedrooms would be scrubbed and dusted and then the gentlemen would return from fishing, trailing mud over the floors and calling for hot water and hot drinks. The servants were not allowed to go to bed until the guests had retired, and that was often at two or three in the morning, but they were expected to be up at six to recommence their labors.

Lucy guessed the staff were normally a happy and easygoing lot of people, but with lack of sleep and work, nerves were stretched to breaking point. Did Mr. Camden ever think of the slavery that went on in his house? wondered Lucy. So many fireplaces to clean out, so much black lead, which, as usual, got everywhere, and no luxury of a hot bath. She was told to remove the black lead from her skin with a little butter.

And all the time, misery ate into her. She often thought she should have had the duke on any terms. But now he had gone. Belinda would be married and she would not be there, for the presence of a ruined sister would cast a shadow on Belinda's day of happiness.

But she was so very tired that during a brief morning break when Mrs. Moreton appeared in the servant's hall and snapped at her, "Present yourself in the drawing room immediately," she felt near to tears.

"I did the drawing room with Betty," wailed Lucy. "We worked and worked. They had drunk toasts the night before and hurled their glasses in the fire, and we spent ages cleaning out the broken glass and scrubbing wine stains off the fender. We—"

"All I know is that you're to go to the drawing room immediately. Mr. Camden's orders," said Mrs. Moreton.

Lucy trailed wearily after her. So far, she had not even seen the owner of this house. Mrs. Moreton opened the door of the drawing room and pulled Lucy inside. Mr. Camden—she supposed it must be he—was sitting in his dressing gown and slippers. He had a guest who was seated opposite him but hidden by the high wings of an armchair.

"Leave us, Mrs. Moreton," said Mr. Camden. "So this is the girl, hey?"

"Yes, this is the girl, and if there are any complaints about her work, then I should hear them."

"No, no, Mrs. Moreton. Off you go."

The housekeeper reluctantly withdrew. "Step forward, miss," said Mr. Camden, getting to his feet. "You may take my chair. You have a visitor."

Lucy went forward and found herself looking at the Duke of Wardshire. She let out a little cry, but Mr. Camden pushed her down into the chair he had vacated and said bracingly, "No hysterics, please. I'll leave you to it, Wardshire."

Lucy looked at the duke, wide-eyed. "What a mess you do look," he said. "What is that black stuff on your cheek?"

"Black lead," said Lucy. "I have been cleaning fireplaces."

He smiled at her in a way that made her tremble. "I got your letter," he said softly. "I did not get it right away or I would never have left here. The landlord found it and sent it on. Did it never occur to you that I might be in love with you?"

"No," whispered Lucy. "Are you?"

"So very much. Now will you have me?"

"Oh, Wardshire, with all my heart."

He stood up and went over to her and scooped her up and carried her back to his chair and set her on his knees. "What fools we have been," he said huskily. "And what a dreadful cap." He took it off and threw it on the fire. "Can you love me a little, Lucy, or would you prefer this life of drudgery?"

"I do love you," said Lucy with a catch in her voice. "That was the real reason, I think, that I did not want to marry you."

He bent his head and kissed her, a long, searching kiss which finally told him that everything he had hoped and prayed for was true. "What now?" asked Lucy shyly, when she could. "Do we go to Gretna?"

"No, my love, we return to Sarsey at all speed so that we may be married at the same time as Belinda. I still have that special license. We will be married and go away somewhere where we can be quiet together. I shall give that poor secretary of mine a holiday. His last problem was that your sister was determined to lead that dog of hers up the aisle. She had even made a white satin coat for the beast. Now, we had better be on our way. But kiss me again first."

Mrs. Moreton hovered anxiously outside the drawing room door. She admired hard workers and had taken a liking to Lucy. She hoped the girl was not in any trouble, but the silence from inside the drawing room was unnerving.

She steeled herself and opened the door. Lucy was lying in the arms of a tall, handsome man whom Mrs. Moreton recognized as the Duke of Wardshire. He was kissing Lucy fiercely and one of his hands was on the girl's breast. Lucy let out a moan and Mrs. Moreton sprang into action.

"Rape!" she screamed. "Rape!"

The couple broke apart and got to their feet as other servants came rushing into the drawing room.

"Duke or no duke, you are not going to seduce one of my girls," shouted Mrs. Moreton. "Men are filthy beasts."

"Control yourself, Mrs. Moreton," came Mr. Camden's amused voice from behind her. "If I guess right, they are to be married."

"Married? A duke marry our Lucy?"

"I am afraid your Lucy has lied to you. She is in fact the duke's fiancée and was playing a trick on him. I must trust to your discretion, Mrs. Moreton."

Mrs. Moreton looked from Lucy's radiant face to the duke's happy one and gave a defiant sniff. "A funny game to me, Mr. Camden."

"Well, I am sure His Grace and Miss Bliss are anxious to be on their way. If you would be so good as to send one of the maids to get Miss Bliss's things and bring them out to the carriage . . . unless you wish to change, Miss Bliss?"

"No," said the duke, replying for Lucy, "there is not any time."

"And may I congratulate you?" asked Mr. Camden.

"Yes, you may," said the duke.

"And must you leave so soon? I could rouse my guests and we could have a party."

Lucy shuddered, thinking of all the work that would mean for the servants as the duke repeated that they must leave right away.

The servants were all gathered in the hall by the time Lucy descended the stairs. She looked round at their tired, strained faces and turned to Mr. Camden.

"I must beg you, sir, to treat your servants better."

"Hey, they are better-paid than most," protested Mr. Camden.

"They are being worked nigh to death by your houseguests," said Lucy. "They do not get to bed until the small hours, and then they have to rise at six. You would not work a horse as hard as they are worked."

"Well, bless my soul. Mrs. Moreton, you should have said something."

"It is not my place to complain," replied the housekeeper, giving Lucy a scandalized look as if Lucy were an uppity housemaid and not the duke's fiancée.

"Never mind," said Mr. Camden. "I'll go easy on them. Send you a present for your wedding. What would you like?"

Before the duke could reply, Lucy said eagerly,

"You could give your servants a holiday. That is a present I would like. They could rest and have a whole day's and a whole night's sleep, which is what they need."

"Done," said Mr. Camden cheerfully. "Mrs. Moreton and Crenshaw"—to his butler—"you may have a whole week off, demme. I'll take this lot up to my box in the Highlands."

Lucy wanted to point out that in that case, the Highland servants would end up with the workload, but suddenly felt too tired to protest. She walked out to the carriage with the duke and climbed wearily in. At least she had done something for her former fellow servants, and knew they would feel grateful to her.

As the carriage drove off, Mrs. Moreton said to the butler, Mr. Crenshaw, "That one will never make a proper duchess."

"Neither she will," agreed the butler. "Playing games acting as a maid and then stepping out of line to get us a holiday. Servants should know their place, and that goes for duchesses, too!"

The journey home for Lucy was a blurred impression of towns and villages as she drifted in and out of sleep, feeling the duke's arms around her in the swaying carriage, seeing the tenderness in his face by the light of the bobbing carriage lamp.

When they reached Sarsey, the duke told her to go to bed immediately and then went in search of Mr. Bliss and his secretary. Unfortunately, Mrs. Bliss arrived when they were discussing the new plans for a double wedding, and she began to exclaim. "Lucy to be married after all! Not ruined! Oh, my stars. The wedding gown. She will need to wear Belinda's. Belinda will just have to have a ball gown made over." She would have gone on for longer if the duke had not told her firmly that Belinda was to wear the wedding dress that had been made for her and that she, Mrs. Bliss, was to have no say in the organization.

Thwarted, Mrs. Bliss tried to go to Lucy's room but found her bedroom door was locked. She searched for Belinda, but Belinda had just been told of Lucy's arrival and the wedding plans and had rushed off to tell Mr. Marsham.

"It's a lot to get ready before tomorrow," said Mr. Marsham doubtfully. "I am so happy Lucy is to wed. Working as a servant! Your sister is a trifle odd, is she not?"

"No odder than the duke," said Belinda cheerfully. "We are all to be married tomorrow and live happily ever after, and nothing can go wrong now."

But things started to go wrong for Lucy that very evening. At first she was radiant as she joined her parents, the duke, and the guests in the drawing room before dinner. Belinda thought Lucy had never looked prettier.

Lady Fortescue and Mr. Graham were among the guests. Lady Fortescue had been delighted when she had heard at first that it was Belinda to wed and not Lucy. Her hopes of getting the duke for herself rose high, and she had been just about to break off her engagement to Mr. Graham when she heard, along with the other guests, about the double wedding planned for the next morning. At first she had congratulated herself on her wisdom in not being too precipitate in ending her engagement to Mr. Graham. But there was something about Lucy's virginal happiness that roused her jealousy and bad temper. As the evening progressed, the desire to dim Lucy's happiness began to burn inside her. Lady Fortescue sparkled and shone as brightly as her diamonds as she tried to focus all attention on herself, and with the exception of the duke and Mr. Marsham, succeeded in doing so, but felt no sense of victory, for Lucy Bliss had not even noticed.

In the drawing room after dinner when the ladies were awaiting the gentlemen, Lady Fortescue saw her opportunity. Lucy was standing by a window, looking dreamily out into the gardens. Lady Fortescue joined her. "So very beautiful, is it not?" she asked. Lucy swung round, her face hardening a little. "Yes, very beautiful," she agreed.

"And soon it will all be yours."

"Yes," said Lucy with a slight air of hauteur. "I will be living in my husband's home, if that is what you mean."

"Such a lucky little girl," cooed Lady Fortescue. "Heigh ho! I suppose I should have accepted Wardshire when he asked me."

"That was so long ago," said Lucy lightly.

"He has changed a lot." There was a waspish edge now to Lady Fortescue's voice. "Ah, we were such innocents once, just like you yourself. Of course, since then, I have been married, and he . . . he has had so *many* women. Not like yourself, of course. I mean courtesans and *experienced* women, experienced in the wisdom of the bedchamber." She fanned herself languidly. "I trust he does not frighten you to death."

"Not as much as you frighten me, Lady Fortescue," said Lucy candidly. "I feel as if something slimy had just crawled over me." She walked past

Lady Fortescue and went to join Belinda and bent down to pat Barney to hide her feelings.

The poison that Lady Fortescue had dripped into her ears was beginning to creep through her whole being. She gave a little shudder.

"Tell me of your adventures," begged Belinda. "We have barely had time to talk."

So Lucy sat down beside her and told her all about being a servant, but when she got to the bit about how she had realized at last that she really loved the duke, her voice faltered. Belinda did not appear to notice.

"I shall be glad when the wedding service is over," she confided, "for Mama is so angry with the duke that she plans to leave immediately. At one point I thought she meant to move into the vicarage. You are suddenly looking a little pale, Lucy. You have had quite an ordeal. Do not worry. Soon you will be alone with your duke."

Alone!

The gentlemen entered the room at that moment. Lady Fortescue went to join the duke. She said something to him and then began to flirt with him in a practiced way. He looked amused.

He will find me boring, thought Lucy, assailed with panic. He is used to women like that. What can he want with a green girl?

But he looked across the room at her and smiled, and she felt her fears drop away and her heart lift again. He loved her, and that was all that mattered.

Anxious to be well rested for the wedding service in the morning, Lucy and Belinda went early to bed. But even on this night, they were not to be spared their mother's presence. She followed them up.

"It is time we all had a comfortable talk," said Mrs. Bliss. "Wardshire and that secretary may think they can handle everything, but it takes a mother to speak to her daughters about *certain* things."

"Such as?" demanded Belinda, sitting down in a chair in Lucy's room with Barney on her lap.

"Tomorrow," said Mrs. Bliss, "you will both lose your virginity. It will be a disgusting and painful ordeal, but it is part of the burden a married woman has to bear."

Both, stricken with embarrassment, looked at her.

"It is best to bite down on something," said Mrs. Bliss. "On my wedding night, I bit clear through the ivory sticks of my fan. Try not to scream too much, for it alarms the servants, and a lady should never scream. Now, I am glad I have put over that distasteful piece of advice in what I pride myself was a practical way." She then began to rattle on about her own gown and how Monsieur Farré had designed it specially, while her daughters sat silently, willing her to go away.

Lucy at last interrupted her by saying if they stayed awake much longer, they would be wrecks on the morrow, and this, thankfully, had the effect of forcing their mother to say good night to them.

When Mrs. Bliss had gone, the sisters looked at each other in dismay. "I don't think I like the sound of what goes on in the marriage bed," said Belinda.

"It's different for you," said Lucy. "Mr. Marsham is bound to be a virgin as well. But what of Wardshire? Hundreds of women in his past, I am sure.

And Lady Fortescue told me that he was only used to women of experience."

"She is a jealous cat who was trying to upset you," retorted Belinda. "Do you know, Lucy, I read in a magazine that it is quite common for a timid bride to ask her husband to wait, perhaps for some years."

Lucy brightened momentarily and then her face fell. "I cannot see Wardshire agreeing to that. I am so worried. Perhaps things will look better in the morning."

But a bright, sunny morning dawned and Lucy's fears rushed back to her, double. She stood like a puppet while Monsieur Farré, who had been up all night with his seamstresses altering one of Lucy's ball gowns, fitted it on her and then darted to the other end of the long saloon that he had commandeered as a dressing room to oversee the fitting of Belinda's gown. Down the length of the long room, the sisters exchanged agonized glances, each still worried to death by what their mother had told them.

Finally they were both ready, and Monsieur Farré had done such a clever job on Lucy's gown that she looked every bit as grand as Belinda, who was attired in a creation of white satin and Brussels lace. Lucy's white and silver ball gown had had the silver trimming ripped off, and now it was trimmed instead with intricate rows of seed pearls and flounces of old lace. She had a pearl choker of four strands round her neck and a pearl and diamond tiara for her head.

The sisters were placed in chairs, side by side,

and told not to move until the bridal carriages arrived at the main door.

They sat like white statues until Belinda gave an exclamation and jumped to her feet. The saloon was on the ground floor with a long stone terrace outside French windows. She had just seen the duke and Mr. Marsham walking past. Belinda jerked open a window and called to them, and they turned about and walked up the terrace, the duke looking amused and saying he thought they were not supposed to see their brides before the wedding.

"We have something to say to you," said Belinda. "Step inside."

"We *can't*, Belinda," protested Lucy in horror.

"I am going to enjoy my wedding," said Belinda defiantly. "I am not going to it frightened to death."

"What has frightened you?" asked Mr. Marsham.

"Mama said—" began Belinda.

"No!" cried Lucy.

"Go on," prompted the duke. "What did Mama say?"

Belinda put her hands behind her back and faced both men like a child about to recite poetry. "She told us that we would find the loss of our virginity a disgusting and painful experience."

A painful blush crept up Mr. Marsham's face, and he covered it with his hands.

"A moment," said the duke coldly. "Come with me, Marsham."

"Now look what you have done," wailed Lucy as the two men walked outside. The duke was talking fiercely to Mr. Marsham. Both waited anxiously, Belinda looking as if she was on the verge of tears.

And then the duke came back. "Go and join

Mr. Marsham in the garden for a few moments, Belinda. I wish to speak to Lucy alone."

Belinda obediently trotted out.

The duke closed the window behind her and jerked the curtains closed and then closed the curtains at the other windows. Then he went and locked the door.

He turned and stood with his arms open. "Come to me, Lucy."

She walked stiffly into his arms and he closed them tightly about her. "You will forget everything your mother told you," he said.

"But—"

"No buts. Just kiss me."

His dark face swam above her own and then his lips came down on hers, hot and burning with all the passion he had previously tried to hold in check. Lucy felt her very bones melt, her whole body seem to fuse with his own, as she suddenly strained against him.

For what seemed the hundredth time, Mrs. Bliss thought she would die of shame. Voices rose and fell at the wedding breakfast, saying they had never been to such a charming wedding, while Mrs. Bliss sat silent, picking at her food.

How could her daughters have behaved so disgracefully? They had both appeared just in time to get into the first of the flower-bedecked wedding carriages. Lucy's tapes were untied, her tiara was askew, and her lips were swollen. Belinda was in a worse state. There were grass stains on the back of her beautiful gown, and mud from the garden on her white satin shoes.

They had not acted as brides should act either.

They had not looked modest. Both had looked triumphantly happy, and they had kissed their husbands in a disgracefully lewd way at the altar.

It was only when the happy couples were ready to leave, Lucy and her duke on the first stage of a journey to Italy, and Belinda and her vicar to their vicarage, that Mrs. Bliss's spirits rose. For one of London's most formidable hostesses, none other than the Countess Lieven, she who often stated, "It is not fashionable where I am not," turned to her and said, "I have never in my life been to a more delightful or well-run affair. I congratulate you!"

And Mrs. Bliss promptly forgot that the now-exhausted Mr. Lewis had arranged the whole thing, and gracefully accepted the compliment before finding her voice again and proceeding to bore as many guests as she could about how she had organized the whole wedding ceremony.

In the best bedroom of an elegant posting house on the Dover road, Lucy watched shyly as her husband prepared to join her in the large four-poster bed. "What did you say to Mr. Marsham?" she asked.

"When, my sweeting?"

"When Belinda called you in from the garden."

"Oh, that." He put one knee on the bed and smiled down at her. "I told him Belinda had bride nerves and that he ought to . . . er . . . warm her cold nerves before the wedding." He slid in between the sheets and reached for her. "Like this," he murmured, "and this . . ."

Lucy stretched languorously against him and sighed, "You are a very wicked duke, after all!"